THE PATH PAST POMASHA

ONE RAINY SEASON IN YUNNAN

THE PATH PAST POMASHA

by BRIAN HERMAN

One Rainy Season in Yunnan: The Path Past Pomasha

Copyright © 2021 by Brian Herman
All rights reserved.
ISBN: 978-1-09839-311-3
eBook: 978-1-09839312-0
Cover Design: Lynne Herman

序幕 PROLOGUE

我也是这样. **Wo ye shi zhe yang.**

These words got me through five years in China. I am like you, whatever it is, I am like you. You like this alcohol? So do I. You're pissed off about something? Yeah, me too. I made a lot of friends this way, and quickly. Everybody likes someone who always agrees. So this is who I strove to be when I lived in Yunnan. I was trying to be the Small Tiger who didn't mess up, and I succeeded—for a while at least.

And while I must admit that my purpose in leaving for China was always to write a story in English, I never at the time suspected the extent to which I would also need to learn Chinese. All those years ago, China was just another mountain to climb, just another girl to kiss, just another dish I needed to taste in hopes of becoming an adventurer. But now, with many years to separate me from the impulsive decisions of my youth, there is a Yunnan of my memories and a Yunnan that I love.

This love, honed during the aughts in the far-flung city of Lime River, allows for this yarn to be woven as seamlessly as possible from Mandarin, English, and all manner of dialectical *Yunnanhua*. It is a story heavily shaded by the personal interactions I had with the regular folk of Lime River, and one that would lead me to a famous tea mountain at the end of the world.

I had many such interactions with the *moto* men who sat outside my apartment building at the International Quadrant in Lime River, so it seems fitting to me that I should start there.

2010

The International Quadrant was the block of apartments near the university where the first foreigners had been kept. It was six floors and three *danyuan*—about 36 units altogether—and there was a water feature out front with frogs and goldfish and the like.

The restrictions on where foreigners could and could not live had since been eased, but I kept my apartment in the Quadrant anyway. It was comfortable enough, and located on a small hill overlooking downtown. It was also the only place in Lime River where even the most conservative locals wouldn't be surprised to find a foreigner.

Every day, without fail, on the sidewalk below my apartment, sat men astride motorcycles. These fellows were farmers who came to the city from the countryside to earn their daily noodle. Rides downtown from the Quadrant cost only three *kuai*, and I often called on the services of the *moto* men to get around town.

It was a Tuesday and the one with the long hair, whose name I knew as Che, was shuffling a deck of cards as he recapped the previous day's winners and losers in the Phoenix Road card game. The others listened intently. One was a balding fellow named Chen. The third was a younger, helmeted bloke who never said much. As I approached, their focus switched from gambling to the prospect of coaxing a fare out of this strange foreigner. As was usually the case, they started talking about me as if I weren't even there.

"*Aiya!*" said Che, the leader: "Here comes the fat American."

The balding one, Chen, threw his head skyward in laughter as an idea came to him: "He's fat because Americans eat only hamburgers and pizza." He kicked at the ground, chuckling, "And all that heat has to go somewhere, right, *right*—?"

"It *is* the bread that makes the American devils so fat," agreed Che. "They aren't like us. They can't eat rice. They can only eat bread. It must be a real pity for them to come here and have nothing to eat."

Chen interrupted to ask, "Remember *Mai-ke*, the first foreigner who ever came here to Lime River? His stomach was big like a drum of cooking oil!"

All three men nodded and laughed, and as soon as I was close enough for a squeeze, Che wasted no time in reaching out to feel the muscles in my arm.

"You're so healthy," he told me.

This was all the comedy that the younger, helmeted bloke, Chou, could bear. Poor Chou had horribly protruding front teeth. He usually hid them in his mouth until he was out on the road, but for now this was too funny and he couldn't resist. Che continued his inspection of my bicep and encouraged the others to do the same.

"I wish I were healthy like you say." I pulled up my shirt and displayed my paunchy, American stomach as they all gathered around, "Maybe I should walk more and take fewer *motos*."

Che and Chen reached out greedily for a rub of my belly, so I continued: "I have been here in Lime River for five years and I still don't look like you. And I've been eating rice too! *Ai-ya!*"

I pounded my abdomen, startling the two grown men playing with the little hairs surrounding my belly button. "Look here!" I said, smacking my tummy. "I will always be thicker than you Chinese. We foreigners are made up of meat and bread, many generations of meat and bread, and that's why we'll always be fat."

This was exactly what the *moto* men wanted to hear, and all three, even the quiet fellow with the buck teeth, resounded in a chorus of, "No! No! You're strong! Powerful like a tiger. Small Tiger—we wish we were like you!"

This was an appropriate time for them to offer me a cigarette. Chen, the balding one, did just that, presenting first pull from his fresh pack of Golden Rooster cigarettes.

I resisted, waving my hands in front of me, saying, "No—no thank you. I'm trying to cut back."

My unmanly response was met with blank stares of bewilderment. This conversation had come to an end.

To make up for it, I chose Chen for my ride and hopped aboard his tiny 50cc *moto*. I ordered: "Take me to Pursuing Pure Perfection."

"Where is that?" He asked.

"Just take me to East Wind Avenue. I can walk from there."

二

There was nothing in appearance to distinguish Pursuing Pure Perfection from any of the other tea houses in Lime River. There were no teak sculptures or Zen fish ponds, no beautiful women in mandarin gowns pouring paper-cup samples. Pursuing Pure Perfection was just one in a string of hundreds of other tea shops lining the first-floor storefronts near the end of East Wind Avenue. *It was sometimes difficult to tell what Pursuing Pure Perfection even was, exactly.* There was never any merchandise in the window, and no sign above the door. Pursuing Pure Perfection was the type of place one would have simply passed right by, fixed instead on some conditional goal in the distance of the ever-changing future. *But many of the world's best locales are like this, aren't they?* They are secrets, known only to locals, or to those with particular, discriminating tastes. Had Pursuing Pure Perfection not been introduced to me by Robert Painter, a man with a passion for the art of Pu'er tea—an avid teacher, student, collector, and purveyor of this delicacy of Yunnan delicacies, I would have simply continued to pass on by, unaware of the universe of tastes and sensations on offer inside this small tea shop.

At Pursuing Pure Perfection, we specialized in the sale of the oldest and most expensive Pu'er tea cakes. A cake of tea is 357 grams of dried and *"fried"* Pu'er tea. The best tea in the world comes from ancient-leaf, old-world Pu'er tea trees, which grow only in certain stretches of remote and mountainous Yunnan. When real, freshly-dried and naturally-fermented Pu'er tea from these regions is pressed into cakes, the individual tea leaves and all of their botanical structures are preserved. Steeping this delicacy of Yunnan delicacies, even many years or decades later, causes the silver-tipped leaves to reconstitute rather magically.

Just pry five to eight grams of tea from your tightly compressed tea cake using a utensil called a tea knife. Then steep with good water at a temperature just below boiling. The color of the broth ranges from golden yellow or sometimes even neon green, to a dark amber or red ochre, depending on how long each cake has been aged and fermented, and the condition of its storage. As opposed to English tea bags, each pot of Pu'er can be steeped multiple times—I've heard even as many as eighteen—with the best steepings usually agreed upon to be the second through fifth.

✴ ✴ ✴ ✴ ✴

The front room of Pursuing Pure Perfection was filled with bouncy crates of Pu'er tea cakes. These crates were stacked one on top of another almost clear up to the ceiling. There were twelve *tong* in each crate, and seven cakes in each *tong,* and everything was arranged in such a haphazard fashion that few visitors actually got any further inside than this front room.

The next room was full of wooden cabinets. These cabinets housed some of Pursuing Pure Perfection's rarest and most expensive aged Pu'er teas. The doors of these cabinets would invariably be left open to invite interest from savvy Pu'er connoisseurs on holiday from Hong Kong, Beijing, or Taiwan.

Past this central room, there was a circular doorway in the ancient style and this doorway led to the tasting room. The centerpiece of the tasting room was a thousand-pound camphor-laurel tree trunk fashioned into an ornate table. It was surrounded by upended stumps from smaller, camphor-laurel trees which were meant for use as stools by customers. On the surface of the camphor table was a cluster of tea paraphernalia, including teapots and hollowed-out gourds filled with every variety of tea utensil imaginable. On the floor behind it sat twenty or so slender terra cotta vases, each one filled with loose tea leaves from a famous tea mountain. And always, at the center of those vases, was Robert Painter—his slim shape and bald head not unlike the smooth and artful earthenware—and his insides surely filled with a comparable volume of tea.

From what I teased out of Robert over a long period of time, I can tell you this: Robert left northern England as a young man and bass player, never to return. His career as a musician led him to the Paris soukous scene, where he jammed with the legendary Lentengo Agube and completed, so far as he saw it, his life's lone ambition. Robert never made it big in soukous, but he was open to possibilities. That led him to Los Angeles, where he painted houses and did odd jobs for ten years, saving a bit and occasionally bringing out the bass guitar on weekends. He acquired a wife, then a divorce, and when he was eventually left with nothing, he boarded a plane for Asia to pursue a life of discipline. Robert Painter was now nearly fifty years old. His mustaches and goatee were dark brown and red, and contained within their ranks not a strand of grey. He dressed exclusively in homespun fabrics, a manner of dress he picked up on meditation retreats in Northern India, where his taste for tea had first been whetted.

"Small Tiger," he said as one of the tea kettles on the table clicked and shut off as it began to boil over, "You have good timing. I was just about to try out this past spring's Bulang Mountain tea."

"Thanks," I said. "I can always use a cup of tea."

Robert nodded in agreement, "Pu'er tea and conversation with like-minded individuals. It's what we all need sometimes." He wiped down the area of the table that had become wet with condensed steam and spillover. "But one cup's not enough. Sit with me and we'll drink three pots—one for the taste, one for our health, and one for our minds and spirits. If you work in the tea shop and drink tea with me, you'll need to drink at least three pots. Otherwise, you may miss the true character of what I suspect will be a thoroughly excellent example of old tree Pu'er tea."

I lit a cigarette, then switched on a small electric fan. Robert had been a smoker in his previous life as a musician, but he didn't smoke anymore. He didn't drink either. And most curiously to me, he never sought out the company of the opposite sex. These were all illusory pastimes, he often informed me, though to his credit, he never criticized me for my ardent pursuit of these glorious vices.

So it was one pot for the taste, one pot for our health, and one for our minds and spirits—and we easily outdrank this prescribed amount by four or fivefold in just that afternoon. We drank teas from Bulang Mountain and from Laobanzhang. We drank older teas and younger ones. We tried the same teas steeped in different pots or with slightly different water.

Eventually, Robert was floating above the camphor trunk, his mind and spirit flushed with pots and pots of Pu'er. He made his way through the circular archway with his head leading his body and his body barely keeping up with his racing head. He stopped briefly in the center room to knock some cakes around. Then he squatted near the bamboo crates in the front room as he began to rummage, presumably looking for a suitable example of whatever particular tea he had in mind.

I smoked and listened as Robert could be heard two rooms away rustling through the bamboo wrappers, muttering about having too much tea. I leaned back on my stool and watched through the archway as bamboo paper rained down into the center of the room. Robert was swearing to himself: "How the hell am I supposed to find anything? Lao Pu and his inventory! No inventory—just piles!"

In point of fact, Lao Pu was the real owner of the tea shop. Robert and I were foreigners and we couldn't own anything; we just sort of hung out at Pursuing Pure Perfection to glean what we could from Lao Pu's vast expertise in the field.

Every so often, we even sold some tea and got paid on commission.

Eventually Robert found what he had been looking for and returned to the camphor trunk with three cakes of tea. He was altogether ignorant of Lao Pu, who had followed him into the tasting room.

"Did we sell any tea today?" Lao Pu asked in a managerial sort of tone.

* * * * *

Lao Pu's hair was cut in the flat-top style popular with middle-aged men from the Northeast. It was stark white and Lao Pu always wore clean, white shirts to match. Lao Pu didn't smoke Golden Rooster cigarettes, preferring instead to smoke his own brand from Shaanxi Province. This all fit in with the general fact that Lao Pu had a condescending air about him, especially when the conversation turned to his native Beijing or to tea. Lao Pu tended to look down on the Lime River locals as poor and uncivilized, as many Chinese from all over China still do. It seemed to me that Lao Pu didn't think too highly of Robert or me either—or of *laowai* in general—but he tolerated us since we were his friends and figurehead foreign salesmen. We were there to attract off-the-beaten-track *laowai* and to maintain the English side of the website. We accepted this arrangement because Lao Pu knew so damn much about tea and because we were so grateful to be in his service. The character "老", or *lao*, in Chinese can mean *old,* but it can also mean *respected and venerable*—and while we called our boss "老" just as we would have any old man in Lime River, our esteem for Lao Pu was as genuine as genuine could be.

"Small Tiger, are you going to sell any tea today?" Lao Pu asked me.

An important rule for social interaction in China is never to give direct answers, especially in the negative. It is far better to answer indirectly or to give no answer at all, a great answer being one that is honest but open to the widest possible range of interpretation—I had no intention of selling any tea that evening—I never bothered selling any tea at the tea shop. So I answered: "Right now I'm studying the subtle differences between Bulang Mountain teas and the ones from Laobanzhang."

This pleased Lao Pu well enough. He noted the many pots of Pu'er spread across the table in various stages of disarray and asked, "So *laowai* can steep tea, too?" Then he leaned over the camphor trunk, inspecting to see which of the shop's rare and expensive teas were being squandered.

To Robert, this was the great insult he was trained to expect from Lao Pu. His face contorted with uncontrollable scorn.

"We're drinking last year's Laobanzhang. Your cup is over there," he pointed brusquely to a teacup he pushed across the table to Lao Pu.

Lao Pu did not sit down. Instead, by merely walking around to the business side of the camphor-laurel trunk, he indicated to Robert that he, Lao Pu, wanted the seat at the center of the table. This was the best seat, the tea-pouring seat—the seat of prime importance—and since Robert knew the rules of being a foreigner in China better than anyone I had ever met, he ceded the position of prime importance, the tea pouring station, to our Chinese boss and tea mentor.

"The Laobanzhang is in this pot," Robert explained to Lao Pu as he abdicated the throne, never forgetting that at Pursuing Pure Perfection, tea was always the object of highest importance.

"What did you think about it?" Lao Pu asked as he inspected the vessel Robert had indicated.

Robert did not answer. He instead pursed his lips together as if deep in contemplation. Then he got up to leave, and I rose to follow.

"Well? What did you think?" Lao Pu asked again as he handed me a cigarette for the road.

"I think it's ageing nicely," I said.

"I wonder where these came from?" Lao Pu ran his fingers over the tea cakes Robert had left behind on the table.

"Oh, out there on one of your piles near the door," Robert shouted back with great pleasure. "You'll find it!"

I shook Lao Pu's hand and said: "Thank you for allowing me to learn about tea in your tea house. I am so happy to be working here. I can't drink tea anywhere else anymore because the tea we serve here is always so superior. I'm really becoming quite spoiled."

Lao Pu beamed with joy. He lit my cigarette and then one for himself before returning to take his seat at the recently-vacated position of prime importance. He raised the teapot Robert had specified, removed the lid and smelled its contents. Then, with a look of youthful intrigue, he set a new kettle of water to boil.

三

If I never sold any tea at the tea shop, you may be wondering how I supported myself in Lime River for so long. But the truth is, any foreigner could earn an easy living in China just by being a foreigner. To Eight Fortunes Liu, I was like jade or silver or China's beloved giant panda. I was a rare commodity with a value nearly unequalled in all of Yunnan. And while it's true that I may have sold a cake or two of tea on my own from time to time, I actually made most of my tea commissions working as a sort-of foreigner-for-hire on Eight Fortune's various technocratic deals.

* * * * *

Eight Fortunes never spent very long with anyone over the phone. He would say:

"Small Tiger, I would like to invite you to dinner tonight at the Golden Rooster Hotel. I'll meet you in front of your building in five minutes."

Eight Fortunes Liu was one of the top executives at the Golden Rooster Tobacco Group—the largest employer, investor, and government entity in Lime River. It was also the sole owner of the Golden Rooster Hotel. This much, at least, is important to note.

* * * * *

Black cloth shoes were a must for this sort of occasion. They were the chosen shoes of Chairman Mao and Deng Xiaoping, and Eight Fortunes appreciated the fact that I got how the whole Communist Party thing worked. He was occasionally being monitored by the party watchdogs to make sure he didn't get *too* big, and these were exactly the types of guys who really appreciated seeing cloth shoes on a fat, subservient *laowai* at these sorts of banquets.

I walked down from my apartment and onto the street, where the motorcycle gargoyles were in the midst of a frenzied conversation. They were in awe of the Audi sedan parked beneath the shaggy palms at the end of the curb. The Audi sedan was the chosen vehicle of the ruling class of Yunnan, and the *moto* men were surprised to see one in such a plebian location.

"Whose do you think it is?" Wondered Che aloud.

"Why is it parking here?" Asked Chen.

The third *moto* driver, Chou, was silent. He slumped languidly over his handlebars with his helmet tipped over his eyes, quite obviously drunk from a recent trip to the canteen.

I approached the sedan quietly, trying not to make a big deal out of something I'd surely be asked to explain for weeks on end during my many *moto* trips downtown. I peered into the heavily-tinted windows. As I did, the doors unlocked and a jealous gasp issued forth from the members of the Phoenix Road Motorcycle Club. *Of course the Audi is here for the fat laowai! For whom else would a member of the Audi Aristocracy be waiting for in front of this building?*

I opened the passenger-side door of Eight Fortune's Audi and entered the tobacco-scented world of the Golden Rooster elite.

四

Eight Fortunes Liu wasn't Han Chinese. He was from the mountains of northern Yunnan near Tibet, where there are at least, I was often reminded, twenty-six recognized and self-governing minorities. We sourced the bulk of PPP's tea from near this region, and if I were to hazard a guess, I would say that Eight Fortunes had the wide face and broad nose of the Duozu minority. The Duozu are a proud people who ruled ancient Yunnan for thousands of years before the revolution, and according to the ancient histories, spread their broad-nosed genes as only warlords can.

Eight Fortunes was a man who verily reeked of the ashes of the most expensive brand of Golden Rooster cigarettes. And as far as anyone in Lime River was concerned, Eight Fortunes Liu damn well oughtta smell that way. It was part of his aura—if not his fragrance of choice, then his fragrance of necessity. Eight Fortunes was the guy who signed the checks for the Golden Rooster Tobacco Group's numerous diversified investments, at home and abroad. These were big checks and people came from all over the world to sit down and deal.

＊ ＊ ＊ ＊ ＊

The leather upholstery inside Eight Fortunes' black Audi was immaculately clean. So was Eight Fortunes' dyed-black hair. The whole drive to the hotel, the dashboard television squawked a taped and redacted replay of an international business news program.

"We're going to the Golden Rooster Hotel," Eight Fortunes reminded me. "The Chinese restaurant, not the Italian one. I have some guests coming in from out of town. We'll be eating in the General Manager's private dining room."

Yes, I had been through this routine many times before with Eight Fortunes. And although I had never been given any specific instructions, I knew from experience what was to be expected. A *laowai* would throw off any of Eight Fortunes' potential rivals. Entertainment vis-à-vis taking shots with a real, live American foreigner would then relieve him from the pressure of being the most sought-after power broker in Lime River. Mr. Liu was the only guy in Lime River who had his own, personal, on-call *laowai*, and for this he was understandably proud.

So why did I do it?

Well, this was one way for me to sell tea without actually having to sell any tea, so I never said *no* to Eight Fortunes. I always jumped at the opportunities he provided, even on short notice. The thing I liked best about Eight Fortunes, was that he was never afraid of questions, as most Chinese were. He was never evasive. If the question was something he couldn't answer, then he just wouldn't. He was at or near the height of his powers, and his position among the most jet-setting of Golden Rooster executives afforded him great freedom in his responses.

"Have you been doing anything interesting recently?" I asked him. This was a very direct question to have asked a superior.

"I was in Beijing from Monday to Wednesday. Then I went to Shenzhen for a few days. I just flew back this afternoon."

"Were you having meetings?" I asked him in a non-specific manner.

Meetings was our own private code for official state business, of which I knew Eight Fortunes would not be able to elaborate upon specifically.

"Yes." He answered.

* * * * *

Eight Fortunes pulled his ruling-class chariot up to the main entrance of the Golden Rooster Hotel and we parked under the porte-cochère; no valet necessary. Never one for wasting time, Eight Fortunes was up and out of the car in an instant and hustling forth to make a grand entrance. I followed as he leaned forward with every next step, his speed never slowing as the doors to the lobby were held open for us by the doorway attendants.

The lobby was built as a tall atrium where any sound was apt to resonate, so each member of the lobby staff, from the concierge to the bellhops, took notice as we walked in the doors. The entrance of Eight Fortunes alone, was enough for them to abandon their duties and provide a rigid stance to attention.

We took the elevator to the twenty-seventh floor—the top floor—and when the door opened, Eight Fortunes and I were met by a hostess wearing a golden vest. She escorted us to a corner room replete with floor-to-ceiling windows, skinny mirrors and flat-screen TVs. These fixtures, plus the Louis XIV-style chandelier hanging over the main dining table, gave the room a gaudy, funhouse effect.

The hostess presented Eight Fortunes with a menu. He opened the heavy, bound volume and began to point and bark orders before turning to me to ask, ever-so-politely:

"What would you like to eat?"

"It doesn't matter. I'll eat anything."

Eight Fortunes turned abruptly to the hostess as she straightened herself nervously. "I'm going to the kitchen to order," he told her. "I want to see who the cook is today."

Then he pointed to a couch near the wall of windows and mirrors and TVs. "You stay here," he told me.

Eight Fortunes shuffled away and the hostess followed, leaving me alone in the room. Several televisions on the walls, like all televisions, were running a news program documenting the economic rise of New China.

I slunk down into that plush hotel sofa and just waited.

五

When Eight Fortunes returned, he was accompanied by a gaggle of golden-vested girls and three new acquaintances. No one introduced themselves or shook hands. Instead, Golden Rooster cigarettes were distributed and lit cordially.

One serving girl had been assigned to each member of the dining party. They waited attentively at our sides, each one holding a single, cloth napkin ready for use. This napkin was redundant, I presumed, as there was already a pile of daintily folded, golden napkins at each place setting. A serving man approached the table and presented Mr. Liu with a platter of raw, marbled beef.

"Japanese Kobe," Eight Fortunes announced to the table. "Yes, this is good," he told the waiter.

The waiter nodded and retired to a cooking station behind a maître d' lectern. There he began to fry the expensive meat on a portable skillet. None of the serving girls smiled. Mine leaned in close to pour green tea. She smelt of sweat. For a moment, the room was silent except for the sounds of the lectern waiter pan-frying the expensive beef.

"Let's drink *Maotai*," Eight Fortunes said to break the silence. He stood and motioned to the hostess to bring over a bottle. "*Maotai* is the best of all Chinese alcohol," he announced, playing to me as if he made this statement for my benefit alone. In fact, I'd drunk *Maotai* with Eight Fortunes many times at banquets such as this, as business required. But you see, Eight Fortunes was simply educating the ignorant *laowai*. I played along with it:

"*Maotai, hmm*? I don't think I've ever had that before. Is it from China?"

The other members of the party all had a good laugh at my expense. Before this, some of the attendees might have been worried about the presence of an unexpected *laowai*. Yet now that this particular *laowai* had proven to be so stupid, they could easily be forgiven for letting their guards down. This was how Eight Fortunes conducted his symphony. Like the drinking of *Maotai*, I had watched it many times. It was for this simple solo that I was paid to play.

"Yes, of course it's from China," answered Mr. Liu. "It is made in the Guizhou province and measures fifty percent alcohol."

The hostess returned and handed Eight Fortunes a bottle. After a cursory inspection, Mr. Liu handed the bottle back to her and nodded to indicate his approval. "These bottles were given to me by the executives from the *Maotai* Group when they came to visit our cigarette factory," he gloated.

The hostess opened the bottle, using a cigarette lighter to melt the limited-edition red wax cap. She poured an adequate quantity of the viscous, clear liquid into Eight Fortunes' shot glass. She then travelled around the circumference of the table, filling the same amount for each guest. With these formalities complete, Eight Fortunes stood to raise his glass. The other members of the party stood with their arms outstretched, with our glasses held high above the table.

My man Eight Fortunes was never one for too much ceremony. He smiled and proclaimed: *"He yi kou," drink one sip*, before tapping the bottom of his glass to the table and taking a long, smooth drag.

The rest of us did the same, and by the time we had finished exhaling our strong, *Maotai* breaths, Eight Fortunes was already seated, chopsticks in hand.

The serving girls brought out the first course on cue. It was the Kobe steak with a black pepper sauce and a garnish of fresh cucumber slices. Then, to accompany the steak, the servers brought out a batch of creamy, shark fin soup, placing the steaming bowls before us at our places.

The Chairman of the Board was the most honored of the guests. His eyes were bright with the clarity that only the independently wealthy anywhere have the time to cultivate. He wore freshly-shined, Italian leather shoes and a tailored sports jacket. His name was Xi, I think, or Xu. He oversaw Golden Rooster's Xiamen office and handled the bulk of Golden Rooster's international trade and investment. If one wanted to get technical about it, he was Eight Fortunes' boss, I think, though Eight Fortunes did most of the heavy lifting. The Chairman didn't smoke Golden Rooster cigarettes, but that's because he didn't smoke at all, and when I'd met him on previous occasions, he'd always extolled the virtues of exercise and clean living. This, I'm quite certain, had nothing at all to do with his favored business practices.

Eight Fortunes toasted the Chairman: *"He yi kou."*

After they shared a drink, the other two men stood up and ventured around the table to toast Eight Fortunes. The first, I found out later, was the Party Secretary of Copper Pot, a town thirty miles southwest of Lime River, but still under Lime River's prefectural authority. The other was a businessman who was building a lodge near a reservoir, halfway between Copper Pot and Lime River.

I was used to these sorts of meetings, and had even been present when Eight Fortunes had financed deals for the local barracks of the People's Army. I was getting better at understanding the proceedings, so I can tell you that the guy from the reservoir needed permission from the Chairman and Eight Fortunes to continue his project on land that was controlled by one of Golden Rooster's subsidiary branches. This was all to the benefit of modern China, of course, but it was also to the personal benefit of all the individuals in the room.

From the way the businessman was dressed, I could tell he wasn't wealthy or powerful. He seemed a little out of his league here in the General Manager's private dining room. He explained discreetly though, that he planned to use his lodge for retreats—the kind of retreats often used by powerful party bosses for business of a delicate nature. Eight Fortunes specialized in this kind of business. He needed places like this lodge to make fully sure that no one could ever keep a full accounting of exactly what he was up to. This included even the Chairman, who wouldn't want to know anything too specific anyway, especially if something did happen that drew too much attention from the bigger party bosses in Kunming or Shenzhen or Beijing.

Where one sat at these sorts of dinners was exceedingly important. I had been placed to the right of Eight Fortunes. The guy who was building the lodge sat to Eight Fortunes' left. The other two fell in line according to rank and *guanxi,* with the Chairman of the Board directly across from Mr. Liu.

…Now, get ready, here we go, because both of the Copper Pot guys wanted to *ganbei,* or *drink to dry glasses,* with Eight Fortunes. He obliged, cordially. Drinks were downed again and again, then refilled each time for us by our napkin servers.

An enormous blue lobster was placed at the center of the table. Someone cut into its shell to reveal its pearly, white flesh. The lobster was flanked by small plates of raw abalone and salmon. A group of uniformed, male servers poured soy sauce into small square dishes in front of us and then topped each dish with a dollop of hot wasabi.

"*He yi kou,*" Eight Fortunes turned to me and clinked my glass.

The hostess opened a new bottle of *Maotai* and the footwomen reappeared, bringing more fish. I grabbed at a piece of abalone with my chopsticks, and then at some sashimi and at a piece of the lobster.

"*Ganbei, ganbei,*" we went around the table, displays of respect all around:

- ✳ *I have a niece. Could you teach her English?*
- ✳ *Mr. Liu, thank you so much for honoring me with your time.*
- ✳ *The Chairman is on the board at over fifty companies—*
- ✳ *Aiya! I never knew foreigners could use chopsticks!*

Then, with our appetites sated and the deal winding down, Eight Fortunes shot up, suddenly remembering:

"And none of you forget to put in an order with Small Tiger for tea—and you'd better order at least one *tong* too," he laughed before downing his last half-glass of *Maotai.* "Then, finally, you may consider our deal complete."

六

No one could say that it wasn't a sun-dappled era in Lime River. Even if you weren't someone like Eight Fortunes, it was still an easy time to get rich or just get by without having to do too much. Families were opening shops and buying automobiles for the first time. The past, the present, and the future, were all rolled into one moment, and I was glad to be there to witness it firsthand.

But still, any foreigner who planned to make a go of it in Yunnan over the long term needed a Lao Pu or an Eight Fortunes or both. This was a Chinese who vouched for you, ensured the renewal of your residence document, and allayed any fear among the local populace that you might, in fact, be a psychopath. Said relationship was never a one-way relationship. The whole idea of it hinged on the dynamic networks of personal influence upon which the whole of Chinese society is based. Favors are exchanged for future favors, and the lesser of any two parties had better take into account the effects their actions have on their superior's personal network. This was an art I was only beginning to learn, but a force that even the simplest Chinese knew as omnipresent and infallible.

One night I was in my apartment when my telephone rang. It was Lao Pu. This was unusual because Lao Pu had never called me before. He usually called Robert. I was preparing for him to ask for a personal favor, but his voice sounded distressed:

"Small Tiger, are you in your apartment?"

"I am."

"No one else is here and I can't get ahold of Lai Sao."

"What can I do to help?"

"I've fallen down outside the tea shop—are you listening?"

"Yes."

"My leg has been injured and I can't stand up. It's really a mess. *Zhen zao gao!* Would you come to the tea shop right away?"

These words set me to action. I threw on my jeans and layered my clothing, and it was a good thing too, because it was cool outside, almost cold. When I arrived downstairs, Che was first in line at the curb.

"I don't have any gas," he told me.

I hopped aboard anyway, and we floated down Phoenix Road together on his bike—two grown men rolling, without gas, into the center of town. I leaned my head back and drifted along with the crisp, tobacco-scented breeze of the evening. Che weaved around a sea of teeter-tottering dump trucks carrying red iron ore to the foundries on the north side of the city. Then he dodged the eddies of the vibrant sidewalk scene, which occasionally, particularly at intersections, spilled out onto the street.

When I hopped off the *moto* at the door of the tea shop, Lao Pu was on his back on the sidewalk, shivering. The door to the tea shop was open, but there was no one inside or anywhere else around. A soft, diaphanous mist hung over this end of East Wind Avenue like an all-encompassing shroud. Lao Pu smiled to see me, but then winced in pain.

"What happened?" I asked him nervously.

"I slipped and fell backwards."

By gesture Lao Pu encouraged me to come take a look at his leg. I could see that his quadriceps was in a terrible state. Soaked tea leaves and shards of glass lay everywhere about him on the cobblestones.

"My thigh muscle has snapped," he said shamefully. "It snapped in half when I fell backwards. It all happened so quickly. Now look at this mess. I've ruined everything."

"Don't worry," I said, as calmly as possible. "I'll take you to the hospital. Do you think you can stand up?"

He tried weakly to prop himself up from the wet and dirty ground.

"I don't think so," he said.

"Just stay here," I told him. "I'm going to call an ambulance."

Lao Pu nodded in agreement.

"Is there anyone else I should call?"

"Please get ahold of Lai Sao. Tell her to meet us at the hospital."

七

The People's Hospital was six crumbling buildings surrounded by a series of interconnected courtyards. When the ambulance arrived, all the courtyards were dark and quiet save one, where the light from the admissions office splashed out onto the drive. As the nurses struggled to unload Lao Pu's stretcher, I was whisked away by hospital orderlies to pay for the ambulance ride. By the time I had completed this transaction, my party had been taken away to Radiology.

It took me a while to find the right building, floor and hallway, and when I finally got to Radiology, Lao Pu was being x-rayed. The same two orderlies from outside were waiting for me at the x-ray unit. They joked with each other excitedly. This was an unusual procedure at such a late hour, they told me. As a result, they would each require ten *yuan* to deliver Lao Pu to his next-up medical services. I paid the orderlies, and when the x-raying was over, they dutifully rolled Lao Pu out of the room, and then out of that building altogether. I followed, thinking it was worth the twenty *kuai* just to know where the hell we were going. I followed alongside the stretcher as it was wheeled down a series of ramps and into the darkness of the courtyards between the buildings.

"Where are we going?" I asked one of the men.

"To Orthopedics," he said.

"Where is that?" I asked.

But he didn't answer, so I just followed as the stretcher creaked and rattled through the otherwise silent courtyards of the soft Yunnan night.

* * * * *

The walls of the Orthopedics ward were painted in nothing more than a layer of thin, white lime. The tile floor was roughly hewn and scuffed. I was relieved to see Lai Sao there waiting for us, and to hear the soothing sound of the quiet strength in her voice. She was on the phone in the hallway, arranging for a doctor, standing beneath the harsh, fluorescent lighting. This wasn't done through the hospital administration, but instead via a series of phone calls to her friends and work colleagues, friends-of-friends, potential friends of the doctors in the Orthopedics department, and friends-of-friends of said doctors. It was a messy process, but one that Lai Sao handled with grace and persistence, as any good woman from Lime River would know how to do. Soon she was even talking to the Number-One-Leader of the People's Hospital on his private cell phone. That call was quick but led to an immediate callback from the chief of Orthopedics, who was at a late dinner, but agreed to come directly to the hospital anyway to attend to Lao Pu's injury.

Lai Sao was the one who brought Lao Pu his rice at the teashop each noon with stir-fried beef and sour bamboo. Her skin was unfortunately sallow, and her eyes were so deeply-set in her skull that one felt as if her soul were on constant display. By her age, nearing forty, any other woman in Lime River would have long ago been married into as high a position as her social status allowed. By that standard, Lai Sao should have been marshaling offspring to and from lessons in piano and English, and supervising their daily completion of hours' worth of primary school assignments. But instead, Lai Sao sat quietly in the tea shop most days after work, keeping to herself. She always helped to wash the teacups once the customers had roistered out for the late-night barbecue stalls with Lao Pu, Robert, and me. Whatever had happened to Lai Sao to prevent the normal course of events in the life of a Chinese woman, it must have been serious. I always wondered about this, but because it would have been far from proper to ask, I never mentioned anything about these curiosities to anyone, not even to Robert.

Robert and I knew only slightly more about Lao Pu. We had, at the tea shop, speculated as to what type of life he must have lived in Beijing before coming to Lime River. Together we concluded that at some point, Lao Pu must have had a family—a wife and at least one child. What had happened to them, no one in Lime River knew, excepting maybe Lai Sao. I wondered if there had been an ugly divorce when divorces were uncommon, or if a fortune was gained and lost. The latter was a common rumor which wafted out from within the caffeinated chatting circles of the other tea shops in Lime River.

I guessed that Lao Pu's unknown past was probably more mundane. He struck me as a lower-middle class Beijinger who had come south to seek a comfortable retirement and the pursuance of a dream. Or maybe that was just my clouded, American spin on things.

Checkered pasts notwithstanding, Lao Pu and Lai Sao made an excellent pair. Their relationship seemed not to be based on money or sex or power, as I thought was the case with most serious Chinese relationships. It was instead based on mutual admiration and adoration, and perhaps, I speculated, upon some complementary details from their pasts, details which they cared to share with each other, but with no one else. And this, to my American sensibilities, seemed natural and right.

八

Each of the sixty patient rooms in the Orthopedics ward had three beds and all the beds were full. Some patients didn't have a room. They lay on cots in the hallway staring up at the ceiling. It was crowded with the families of the patients and all the nurses milling about, bumping into each other while performing their caretaker duties. The worst part was that every patient's call button rang Beethoven's *Fur Elise*. The electronic rendition clamored on incessantly over the intercom system. Every time. Every call. *Fur Elise* this and *Fur Elise* that. Beethoven was the soundtrack for the days and nights I was to spend in the Orthopedics ward with Lao Pu.

The chief of Orthopedics arrived not long after his phone conversation with Lai Sao. He was a short, sweaty man who spoke a little English. He greeted Robert and me in the jostling crowd that had gathered in the hallway to watch what the hell two foreigners were even doing there; then he sought out the woman with whom he had spoken over the phone. After his consult with Lai Sao on the state of affairs, he made his way to see Lao

Pu at the center of the throng. Lai Sao presented the doctor with the X-ray film from Radiology and he held it up to the florescent lighting on the ceiling to get a better look.

"There," he said, pointing. "See there."

Members of the crowd all around craned their necks and elbowed one another for a better view. Lai Sao scolded them: "This is none of your business. Don't you have something better to do?"

Most stared back blankly. A few, but not many, bowed their heads guiltily and walked away.

"Go away!" Lai Sao flicked her hands at the rest. "Go somewhere else. Please give us some privacy."

The crowd dispersed slowly, but not entirely. Lai Sao turned to the doctor, who, oblivious to all the commotion, had continued his thorough analysis.

"The muscle here is completely torn," he said. "All four of the quadriceps muscles *here* have snapped. The patient will need surgery to reconnect them."

Robert looked at me and jeered to indicate the seriousness of the situation. Lao Pu, motionless and silent on the stretcher until now, sighed deeply.

"Will you do us the honor of performing the surgery?" Lai Sao asked the chief of Orthopedics with the utmost deference and humility.

"The surgery cannot be performed until tomorrow," the chief replied sharply, stepping backwards and shaking his head from side to side.

"But you are here now," pleaded a distressed Lai Sao. "I know it is late and we are a great trouble to you, but if you would please do us the honor of performing this surgery yourself—we have heard so many people speak highly of your expertise."

"Tomorrow morning," the chief insisted, taking another step back and shaking his head, the sweat from his temples now reflecting the fluorescent lighting in a manner most unappealing.

Lai Sao moved in, not taking *no* for an answer, and I heard her ask oh-so-delicately if she could speak to the chief in private. To this he agreed, and he led Lai Sao into the privacy of the nurses' station.

Later I heard that Lai Sao had pressed the chief on the issue of immediate surgery, displaying the same tenacity she had shown in dispersing the crowd of onlookers in the hallway. In private, the chief admitted that, although he was still the head of the department, he was old, and, at present, his position was mostly honorific. On top of this, his duties as chief frequently involved social occasions involving alcohol, and nowadays his hands shook terribly when he tried to operate. He suggested instead his second-in-command, Doctor Zhang, who was younger, had been trained in Shanghai, and was usually not drunk.

For his insight, the chief of Orthopedics then accepted a token of a few thousand *yuan* from Lai Sao. This exchange was performed quickly and neatly by two people who knew well their positions in society, both with a deep and unwavering understanding of how things worked. A moment later they emerged from the nurses' station to make an announcement to the crowd that had once again gathered around Lao Pu's stretcher in the hallway:

"The surgery will be performed tonight!"

The sweaty chief pushed his way through the crowd, saying, "Back away, back away—go and tend to your loved ones." He stopped above a pathetic Lao Pu, still lying meekly on his back, and said, "Doctor Zhang is on his way. He is my second in command. Zhang is young and has been trained in Shanghai. He is going to perform surgery to reattach your quadriceps muscles. Do you agree to this procedure?"

Lao Pu nodded solemnly in the affirmative.

"Good," said the chief, who was growing sweatier and sweatier, swaying in the bad light. "We will begin in a half an hour."

Doctor Zhang arrived in exactly that amount of time, and when he did, Lai Sao was there at the door waiting for him, making sure he was indeed young and well-trained and definitely not drunk. Lai Sao was grateful to Robert and me, but also a little embarrassed and flushed. Lao Pu and Lai Sao weren't married, so this was a shameful situation to be happening in public. As Dr. Zhang donned his white gown and scrubbed in for the procedure, Lai Sao insisted that Robert and I go home. "This will help to disperse the crowd," she finally convinced us, but only after we promised to visit early again the following morning.

九

The surgery was more or less a success, and afterwards, Lao Pu was assigned to a room directly across the hallway from the nurses' station, where the din of electronic *Fur Elise* resonated each time the nurses ran to and from their duties. It was a clamorous location, but better than being stuck out on a bed in the hallway somewhere, I reasoned.

Pu's room was inhabited by two other patients and their family groups. The patient in the center bed was a young man from the Lime River countryside who had taken a nasty fall from his motorcycle. His head was wrapped in a bloodied bandage. It seemed he had sustained some sort of traumatic brain injury in the fall. His mother and father paced around the room nervously pointing out things they hoped he would recognize: his younger sister, a pack of his favorite cigarettes, a picture of their family's house. The patient smiled widely and enthusiastically at the amusement but was far more impressed by the presence of the *laowai* in the room. The moment his minders left him, he stood next to my chair, poking at me, and every so often giggling to himself.

The patient on the far side of the room near the window was in a terrible state. A tube led from her stomach down to the floor. She was sweating profusely, barely able to turn away from the tumult created by her brain-damaged neighbor. She had undergone four spinal surgeries, none of which had been particularly successful. I watched as her melancholy husband tended to her with extreme care and humanity. He smiled and made small talk in dialect when he felt able, but most of the time he just sat and blotted the sweat from his wife's forehead with a wet cloth, or gazed out the window looking forlorn.

In the first week of Lao Pu's extended hospital stay Lai Sao, Robert and I set a schedule between ourselves to care for Lao Pu. I was happy to have a little responsibility, and I took it as a chance to learn some medical terminology. Sometimes my time at Lao Pu's bedside lasted an hour, sometimes it lasted all day and into the night. It depended on Lai Sao's shifts at the Public Safety Bureau, and Robert's rather non-existent work schedule. It didn't matter to me. I was always available to pick up rice and vegetables from a reputable canteen. Eight Fortunes hadn't called me for a while. He was probably off making deals in booming East Coast places like Guangzhou or Xiamen or Shenzhen, and I was otherwise unencumbered.

In those faraway places as well as in Lime River, tropical summer moisture from the southern seas was on its way back northward. I could feel it as the hemisphere tipped its way back from winter, click by click, ever so slowly. When we weren't at the hospital tending to Lao Pu, Robert and I sat in the tea shop drinking tea with the door propped open and the fan on for ventilation. We were under strict orders to keep the shop running just in case any cash-flush tourists happened to show up. Both Robert and I knew this would be unlikely during this time of year—the rainy, summer season—but we kept the shop open anyway, if only to inform Lao Pu of the minutiae of each's day's events, hoping that the knowledge of our daily business endeavors would help to fortify his strength.

One night when Lao Pu was sleeping soundly I took over the watch from an exhausted Lai Sao. I took this opportunity to examine the post-operation x-ray. I could see where Dr. Zhang drove three heavy metal screws into Lao Pu's patella to reattach the torn tendons. *Ouch.*

Just then, as if he felt me wincing, Lao Pu awoke in a great deal of pain…he very quickly began to wail.

Inpatient care at hospitals in Yunnan is almost non-existent. After a surgical procedure, the patient is more or less left to fend for themselves. The nurse visits the room a few times a day to take an axial temperature, but that is where the hospital services for a recuperating patient end. Despite this uncomfortable truth, I called for a nurse.

"There is no need for a man to suffer like this," I remarked in a flustered sort of way as I pleaded for the strongest dose of pain medicine available.

The nurse who answered had a well-placed beauty mark above her red, heart-shaped lips. Of this attribute, I could tell she was immensely proud. In a country of a billion and a half people, this was something, at least, that made her stand out. Like the other nurses, she wore a blue deaconess cap—but she was the head nurse, and she informed me quite crossly:

"Pain is the only way to heal. No patients here are to be prescribed any pain medication, no matter the ailment, by order of the administration."

"I want to speak to a doctor," I demanded, not waiting for a response, instead stomping my way across the hallway to the nurses' station to press the issue myself.

When I got there, there was the chief of Orthopedics, that same sweaty English-speaker—the one who had arranged for Lao Pu's surgery with all his artful maneuvering. I greeted him and asked him to make a special exception on the morphine for Lao Pu. "*Mafeng?*" I guessed at the transliteration for the word *morphine*.

He furrowed his brow and shook his head from side to side.

"*Ma-Feng*," I tried again, this time more slowly. "*Zhi teng de*—something to ease the pain."

"Oh!" The doctor smiled, suddenly realizing what I was trying to say.

"*Ma Fei, Ma Fei*," he answered, correcting me. "I understand." He nodded his head triumphantly. Then he stopped short and shook his head from side to side. "We have none of that here," he said plaintively.

"Can we get some from somewhere?" I asked. "I think my friend really needs it."

He just shook his head. "Not in all of Yunnan, not even in Kunming."

"Have you anything that's even close? I don't care if it's not that strong. I know opiates are not commonly used here these days, but surely you must have something?"

"No. There is nothing I can do. There has long been a shortage of medicines here in Yunnan."

＋

Summer came, and brought with it the rains, the uninterrupted patter of raindrops pelting the tin roofs of the buildings surrounding my apartment in the International Quadrant. One after another, these days stayed grey all day, every day, the light in the sky never graduating beyond the first ashy hues of dawn. During the rainy season, the roosters did not sound their morning reverie. The feline quotient of Lime River did not descend to the courtyards for their usual, boisterous lovemaking. All was quiet save the delicate cascade of slick silver streaming from the rooftops of the Quadrant to the muddy ground below. The rain lasted for hours or days and I was lost to the world.

I used this solace for the betterment of myself. I had grown older and more deliberate. I stayed inside, brushing strokes and characters in preparation for a future in which I might not have the opportunity to do so. I quit smoking by rolling pinners fashioned from Cuban cigars taken from Eight Fortunes' banquets. During the days, I tossed and rocked and swayed as if I were dozing in the cabin of a mighty ship. At night I slept but little, sweating without sheets in the humid air of the apartment. But after a time, when the storms of addiction had abated, I emerged from my quarters new and fresh and delicate—sharp with the knowledge from my study and thirsty for life. Often, after a late afternoon nap, I made it no further than the tea shop, where the warm lighting and open doors once again started to draw familiar faces back to drink Pu'er and chat in the rainy summer twilight. If there happened not to be any customers, Robert and I sat at our stations by the trunk, busily preparing the website graphics and linkages that would propel Pursing Pure Perfection into the information age.

Meanwhile, Lao Pu began to grow restless in the hospital. He resented everyone seeing him in his weakened condition. He started saying strange things, demanding that Robert and I climb to the top of Longshen Mountain to find a tea that was magic. He repeated his mantra again and again, and again and again. So much so, that even Robert started to consider this plan's merits as a valid treatment option.

"Tea won't cure a thing like that!" I blurted back.

Robert sighed in retort, his bony shoulders slumping down in his thick, hempen sweater. He said:

"Chinese medicine puts a lot of stock in the healing properties of things." He ladled some water out of a gourd on the floor and into one of the many kettles on the camphor trunk. "If Lao Pu believes that this tea from Longshen Mountain will help him heal, well then I'm apt to believe it too. A man needs hope, you know." He then gave about as much of a harrumph as a hemp-wearing Buddhist can do, before adding, "There's plenty of it up there. Lao Pu says we just have to meet with one of his associates at the base of the mountain. The healing properties of Longshen old tree Pu'er tea are world-renowned."

I shook my head in a disbelieving sort of way, but as I hadn't ever turned down an opportunity for adventure yet, I relented and agreed to go. In the interest of Lao Pu's health, it was decided that we should set off from Robert's house the very next afternoon.

Robert grinned his best all-knowing, deep-happiness smile:

"Well, what should we drink to prepare us for this journey?"

十一

The next day, the unified front of the national sorting movement dispersed into a multitude of smaller bands as they exited the factory gates. This was one shift of tobacco sorters from the roasting plant—relocated villagers, all of them, proudly adorned in the beige uniforms and communist-style baseball caps of the lowest caste of the Golden Rooster community.

The men lit cigarettes and called to each other: "Meet us in the Golden Flavor Canteen!" Here, they gathered around circular tables with family-style bowls heaped with steaming greens. From small glass bottles, they poured full glasses of *baijiu* and toasted one another as if it were Saturday night on the French Riviera, and not Monday afternoon along Phoenix Road's river of used cooking oil and slime.

The women held hands and clucked like egg-laying hens as they decided what to eat. Those opting for cold rice noodles barked their orders over the greasy counters at the ladling ladies of noodle heaven. Others purchased cellophane baggies of fried potatoes or stink tofu from the streetside vendors, all of whom could be seen dumping hot wokfuls of cooking oil into the abysmal gutter refuse of that day's business endeavors.

It was a hot afternoon so I took a narrow alleyway from the factory across town, through Old Lime River. This was the heart of the city, the pulse of the past, still standing and breathing, safely hidden behind the wide avenues and plasma-screen advertisements of the modern experience. The sunlight had splashed itself high against the mud-brick walls here. Beset by this onslaught of radiance, the walls baked and cracked and groaned with age. These walls were being broken down by the sun into the sand of their making, sending specks of shimmering earth to dance in the sunlight. The back kitchens of a thousand noodle houses sang in a chorus of metal spatulas scraping industrial-sized woks; porcelain bowls chimed against glass in vast, soapy washbasins. Thick smoke from the charcoal braziers filled the air, coalescing with the crumbling dust from the walls.

A stream of electric wires ran haphazardly above—hundreds of tributaries forming one vast river of electricity. Every so often, one of the wires darted seductively into a hole in the mud stucco, delivering a taste of the modern life—a television connection, hot water, a simple space heater—to a modern family living inside. I followed the corridor, arms half-extended, my fingertips running along the walls to either side in chorus with the wires, loosening and returning via a poetic, floating downfall, tiny particles long ago separated from their mother, the Earth.

After many such meandering corners, I came across a small, golden dog resting in a sunny spot. This dog made no objection to my offense upon his space in Old Lime River. He lay instead upon the dusty ground with his forelegs aft, head held high, watching me with unmoving, black eyes of no discernable attitude. As I passed, the dog remained in position, steadily watching the direction from whence I had come as if I had never been, as if no one had ever been, and as if he himself was composed of the fallen dust from the ancient walls, having given up on the impermanence of life and been blessed, reincarnated as a holy being—the Guardian of Nothing.

The space between the walls grew wider. The mud houses on either side grew taller. Black wrens with opalescent plumage warbled in wicker cages next to ornate, wood-framed doorways. With a flourish, the birds whistled shrill, imitated cries through their dilated throats, defying the Guardian of Nothing and his realm and announcing my return to the modern world at the small intersection ahead.

Here, the mud brick walls gave way to stalls bursting with spice. Pungent aromas of chives and garlic sprung from the market tables as women in straw hats misted and arranged their greens. I continued along the path, through the stalls and carts, until a man with tousled hair blocked my way:

"Selling green vegetables!" he announced loudly to the crowd, but mostly to me. "Selling green vegetables!"

He had stacks of kale and bulbous heads of cabbage and cauliflower. Another tabletop vibrated in the red and green bursts of Yunnan's famous hot peppers. Nearby, a woman sold eggs for five *jiao* a piece from a wicker basket lined with straw. There was a man stacking a pyramid of severed fish heads; the fish leaked their essence into a stream on the path. Then the world of slithering black eels, and further, vats of golden honey with floating icebergs of honeycomb. Confused bees kept guard, ignoring the sleeping offspring of the potato wholesalers. The children, faces dusty from play, slept peacefully on the sacks of potatoes as their parents tended to their stock beneath the shade of large, family umbrellas.

It was too hot to linger for too long in the southern sun. I began to sweat. The wind picked up and sent a few of the vegetable wholesalers chasing after their oversized umbrellas. Another gust and I heard the chimes and bells of the Drum Tower sing a delicate melody. I followed the eerie serenade, then turned to make my way down to the river.

十二

Robert's distinctive house was nestled in a grove of banana and *Ficus* trees in a low-lying spot along the floodplain of the Mekong, almost directly below the impressive spans of the New Bridge. The New Bridge, as people called it, was a high and presumptuous bridge. At night it shone ever-brightly, and was a testament to large things being built quickly with all the new money in China, and, yes, even in the wild borderlands of Yunnan. The New Bridge *was* important. It connected Lime River to Kunming to the rest of mainland China to the rest of the world, and in that order precisely. Heading out of Lime River in any other direction would take you only as far as the jungles of Laos or Burma or Vietnam.

That afternoon I reached the banks of the Mekong to find Robert sitting in his doorway, meditating. A brown prayer shawl was draped over his shoulders and he altogether looked like a great, white Lama, bald and aloof, eyes closed and completely at peace. He sat perched atop a blue prayer cushion, an authentic one that only a hardened, Southeast-Asia *laowai* would be likely to possess. I didn't want to interrupt the Lama, so I left my backpack next to him on the dilapidated veranda and headed down the path through the bushes to the Mekong.

There were a few other Flower-Belt style shacks between Robert's house and the river. These were curious places. Mostly they were used as brothels, having long since been abandoned as places for Flower-Belt families to live and farm the fertile river banks. The women now stood on porches with the pink and purple parasols that were the symbols of their trade. In the scraggly bushes, one could see the jerky movements of bodies intertwined. Motorcycle drivers and day laborers, their faces black from decades of hard work in the sun, stood triumphantly behind distracted looking girls. One of the men came out from behind the bushes, tugging up at his trousers. A dark-skinned girl with long, black hair followed, cleaning her teeth with her index finger. The man slapped me on my back. He was flushed and smiling broadly. "You go next," he recommended.

* * * * *

I walked to where pools of clear water and red sargassum blocked my path. I waded through the tidal deposits, wetting my sandals. The pools opened into broader channels here; each channel siphoned its portion of the river and sent it rushing down lyrically towards Laos and Burma. The flow was turquoise and uncontrollable, still strong at times despite the Golden Rooster Group's construction of the hydroelectric dam upriver.

Local youths with black, spiky hair drove their motorcycles into what was left of the mighty river, cleansing their bikes of the dust from the constant construction on this side of town. Old men fished in the smaller of the channels, using long nets and catching a few finger-long fishes per cast. The prostitutes, too, came down to the river for a wash. Their white-shirted pimps trawled the riverbanks, looking menacing and whistling at potential customers. I skipped stones and cooled my feet in the water as the cars and trucks on the New Bridge rattled on in an endless parade.

After a time, I walked back to Robert's house, intent to rouse him if I needed. But he was already there waiting for me, standing next to his rucksack on the porch, conscious but still silent and aloof. So we just walked together, neither of us speaking, up the dirt path to the bus station.

十三

If this was the adventure I had been seeking, it began somewhat inauspiciously at the North Bus Station, which was nothing more than a collection of squat, whitewashed buildings surrounded by a large, paved parking lot. The main building stood in the absolute center of the parking lot and housed the ticket office. To the right and left there were shops where one could buy peanuts, convenient noodles, beverages, preserved meats, cigarettes, and all manner of sweets and potato chips. Above these small *maibu*, on the second story, was a horribly dingy dormitory, visible from the parking lot, presumably for bus station employees of low rank. Behind each of these doors lived a bus station employee, who slept and awoke to the harrumph of diesel engines and the aroma of tailpipe monoxide mixed with that of the passengers' and drivers' hastily smoked cigarettes.

Another squat building served as a restaurant serving to-go bowls of white rice with portions of basic meat and vegetables. The bus drivers waited the minutes it took for water closet breaks, or to add a few more passengers, or to negotiate the shipment of some cargo, then the buses drove off to points along the yet-unfinished Pan-Asian Highway. Robert and I were the only *laowai* there, and it must have looked like we wanted to go somewhere, because we were at once besieged by hawkers, who followed us as we made our way toward the ticket window.

Soon they were pressing their bodies into ours, bleating their incessant cries:

"Where are you going?"

"Where are you going?"

Robert wasn't interested in haggling. He didn't give a damn about where he sat. He'd lived in India and could handle anything. So he excused himself to use the restroom and left me there to deal with the touts myself.

One hawker with a fat head was more aggressive than the others. "Where are you going?" He pushed his face into mine to continue the salvo. "Where are you going?"

Don't talk to him, I thought. Don't even look him in the eye. Pretend you don't understand. *Walk. Just walk. Go toward the ticket booth.*

"Where are you going?"

"Where are you going?"

Keep walking. Don't make eye contact. Don't even look.

"You are French. Welcome to China, Mr. France," the tout broke into almost unintelligible dialect as he started to buy that I didn't understand and slipped into his everyday speech patterns. But the French part caught me off-guard. *French?!* And I must have nodded slightly involuntarily in the negative, only catching myself once the damage had already been done.

52

"Oh! You're not French," guessed the tout. "Maybe American then, maybe English. It's ok. *No pobrolem.* Where are you going, American? I'll get you a good price. A cheap price."

I gave up the rouse of not understanding, perhaps too easily, and asked, "For which bus? I want to take the express bus. I don't want to take a small bus."

"Yes. Yes. The Express Bus. Very Fast. Where are you going?"

"To Pomasha. Near Longshen Mountain."

"Yes. Yes. Longshen *Shan.* Very Fast. Night bus. You sleep. Rest." The man turned his chubby, little head sideways and rested it on a pillow made with his hands. Then he popped his head up suddenly, saying, "Wake up in Longshen Shan." He smiled confidently, completely unaware of the bits of green vegetable stuck between his teeth from a recent trip to the canteen.

"Which bus?" I wanted clarification.

"The best one."

Oh brother, I thought. This guy's a liar. The touts never hawked tickets for the express buses. The express bus tickets sell themselves. The tickets the hawkers push are for the slower, older, driftier tier of previously-owned buses, often illegal, which pull over at every opportunity to pick up roadside travelers.

"I want a window seat," I said.

"*No pobrolem*," He said. "There are eight window seats left."

"But only if you can assure me a bed with a window that actually opens," I made sure to add. "And the seat next to it for my friend."

"Yes, I understand." The tout nodded excitedly. "You like the window. *No pobrolem.*"

"Ok. It's a deal," I decided as I handed the man a paltry amount of money for what was to be a trip of eight or nine hours for two people. The tout bade me to follow and led me eagerly to the ticket counter where he proudly proclaimed that he had sold a ticket to the *laowai*. Once his boasting was complete, the money was exchanged and the tout was handed two tickets by the official woman behind the glass. He then handed the tickets over to me and waved me off decisively to wait for his commission.

"Go. Go." He said. "The window seat—just like you wanted. Go now. The bus will be leaving soon."

As soon as I looked at the ticket to see the assigned bay, I knew. Hiding there, behind two luxury liners, I saw exactly what I had been dreading—a small, blue and grey coach, half the size of the others. It was a metallic loaf of bread—a breadbus!"

"No. No. No," I said rapidly, repeating myself in a manner most Chinese. "This isn't what I wanted," I turned back to the tout and squared up defiantly.

But my tout and all the others just eyed me triumphantly.

"I'm going back to the ticket counter to buy a ticket for one of the big busses," I said peevishly.

My tout, his commission in hand, put his hand on my shoulder consolingly, "There are no window seats left on the big buses anyway. All of those tickets sold out this afternoon."

Robert then came out of the bathroom, yanking up at his trousers. He took his ticket without even looking and climbed aboard the breadbus, saying nothing. He was smiling wildly and maniacally, no doubt excited for the trip ahead. I gulped and followed him up the narrow gangway, and as we walked back to the last row of rickety bunks, the breadbus departed. It labored to climb the on-ramp of the Pan-Asian Highway, chug-chug-chug-ging, panting away.

We were in a rush to find the magic tea for Lao Pu, to be certain, but as you may have already noticed—things in Yunnan never tend to unfold quickly—so that night on the bus I couldn't help but to relish the time—

The bus turned northwards, through the darkness of night. Headlights from other vehicles shone in through the back windows, some soft and yellow, some harsh and white. The echoes of this illumination bounced across the ceiling of the bus like rolling waves of sand in limpid blue water. When we were between cities, there were stars. I watched out the window at the inky, black darkness of the Yunnan, jungle night. A giant crab constellation shone down upon the terrain. It spun and danced its sideways-walking dance across the sky as my vessel, the breadbus, now humming smoothly, picked its way up to still higher altitudes of the Yun-Gui Plateau; up, up, up, one long sweeping curve after the next, the small loaf of bread shooting at speed through the creases between the mountains, like a child's toy in an oversized world of papier-mâché and pipe cleaners.

The other passengers, silent in their narrow bunks, slept soundly as the bus keeled and bowed, slipping through tunnel after tunnel before emerging from the bowels of yet another mountain; the passengers' motionless bodies, fixed in place and time as everything—the bus, the highway, the stars and sky—revolved around them gyroscopically. Everything was still save our progress towards the goal—I slept.

十四

It was the stillest of still when the bus arrived in Pomasha. It made its stop at the local Tourist Bureau and left us standing there in the empty street. Pomasha was a tiny market town at the base of a long range of mountains. The Tourist Bureau was shuttered and there were only a few other shabby buildings around. I was groggy with sleep and said nothing. Robert was likewise groggy, having not meditated since the night before. Neither of us spoke, and we just kind of stood there wondering dumbly what to do.

Suddenly, an object buzzed somewhere near the top of the mountain. It was swooping around the bends like a swallow in flight, kicking up dust. The way it moved against the majestic backdrop was altogether exhilarating, and now that it was closer, I could make out that it was a black sport utility vehicle, shiny and new. Robert and I just watched it—it was the only thing moving for miles in any direction. And when the SUV eventually pulled to a stop in front of us at the Pomasha Tourist Bureau, Robert stepped in front of me and peered in through the driver's side window.

"Lao Song?" he inquired, hoping to find our connection for the magic tea. I couldn't quite make out the response, but Robert gave me a nod in the affirmative before he climbed into the front seat. Then I opened the door behind him and slunk into the sticky, leather interior of the back. The air inside the car smelled robustly of Golden Rooster cigarettes.

Had they resided in the same place at the same time, Lao Song and Lao Pu may have been mistaken for brothers. Song was a less-sophisticated version of everyone's favorite tea guru. He was a serious Han Chinese who'd made his money in dealing Myanmar border jade. He now kept various other interests in Pomasha, including a stake in the magic tea that cured all, or so Lao Pu had assured us. Song had a Flower-Belt fiancé from the village at the top of the mountain, and it was through these relations that he was able to lease the bottom half of the mountain from the Flower-Belt elders to grow his profitable banana and rubber trees.

And then it was ZOOOM as the car rounded the first bend into Longshen Gorge. This was the first turn in the Yangzi River, the Long River, the River of the Golden Sands. Here rushing, glacial water began its long and arduous path through the Sichuan basin, and across the Yangzi plain, all the way to the Lake District and Shanghai, some four-thousand miles away. But not us—

We were in the ancient world of watercolor scrolls, where rice paddies spilled down the mountains like pools of rich lacquer shimmering on an artist's table in the sun. Men up and down the steep inclines plowed their fields atop water buffalo. They sat bareback on their beasts, with both beings trudging together through the mud.

Women passed with long, braided hair. They carried yokes on their shoulders holding bundles of bamboo, chickens in cages, or water in jugs. These were beautiful, strong women, and it bothered me slightly that Lao

Song might just crash his vehicle into any one of them. Yes, Lao Song was a crankier, grimier version of Lao Pu. He was concerned only about grinding his vehicle up the mountain with his shoulders hunched over the steering wheel.

"How is Lao Pu?" He asked Robert, irritably.

"He is somewhat ok," Robert answered in a roundabout sort of way in Chinese.

Lao Song listened and nodded and dragged on his smoke. When Robert was done, Lao Song began to talk about his business. It was clear he wanted us to know that he was a big man around these parts. Robert listened respectfully and then gave his two cents on the tea business.

I gazed out the window at the Yangzi River as it dove into the ever-receding core of the gorge far below. It was icy blue down there where the water pounded into the chasm with all the force of the Himalaya. And our tiny SUV got eaten up by the immense scenery of it all and I was gone. I remained this way, thoroughly contented, until the car stopped abruptly. Here, one of the lacquered waterfalls had chosen to alter its course to block our way.

"Ok," said Lao Song, after we'd all gotten out of the car and had a chance to inspect the situation. "The trail to Lotus Blossom Village and the tea from Longshen Shan is just up there."

He pointed up the road three yawning bends, to a thick patch of foliage between two folds in the mountain.

Robert and I thanked him for the ride and the directions. Lao Song just kind of shrugged solemnly. He returned to his vehicle and hunched over the steering wheel. There, he lit another cigarette, took a long drag and began trudging the SUV back down the mountain toward Pomasha.

"Well, he wasn't really one for long goodbyes, was he?" Robert asked with a chuckle.

十五

With the utmost in whimsy, my Buddhist friend traversed the falls, stepping first over the rocks which had come down with the slide, then over the rush of cascading blue water. I hopped over too, looking long at the steep side of the gorge, craning my neck to get a better view of the top. We meandered the three long curves in the road as prescribed by Lao Song, then stepped off the road and into the jungle at the spot where our guide had instructed.

The forest grew up all around, erasing us from the here and now and sending us hurtling into a broader swath of time. Large, square cobblestones jutted out at odd angles. The ruts between them became peppered with goat droppings. Robert bounded from stone to stone, pouncing from one side of the trail clear on over to the other. The steep incline started here, and it siphoned my young, strong body right up into its tunnel of drenching, vine-soaked trees.

Soon we could see the gorge stretching out below us, more and more majestic as we rose. Diamond rivulets painted themselves down the mountain, from nook to nook, sometimes crossing the trail. These cascading streamlets brought with them the fertile soil from the top of the mountain, bit by bit—soil from the community of mountaintop gatherers brought down from Heaven to the Earth—and let's not forget, to Lao Song to fertilize his profitable banana and rubber plantations. In this place, flying faery butterflies still flitted about, and all manner of beetles and dragonflies displayed their wondrous trinkets. Tea bushes started popping up here and there and Robert was at once exceedingly interested. "This is bush tea," he said. "We don't sell any of this stuff at the shop." He tilted his head back to see if I was listening before adding, "but it gives farmers at lower elevations some tea that can be sold at market."

We now found our way into a much deeper tract of jungle, one tucked far and away from the main cleave of the gorge. The path which bound us clung to a crease in the tectonic, crackling Earth. Delicate orchids clung precariously between the boulders. Climbing vines drug fruit and melons along the trail at our sides, and then up again into the tall, tall trees. The air grew thin as we hiked, higher and higher, until—quite to our surprise—a lively chap came bounding down the path.

"*Aiya*! Two real foreigners," he exclaimed as he stopped before us and angled in for a better look.

This man was something of a quirky fellow. He was village thin, wore a flower-belt, and there was a medicine gourd dangling around his neck. Even after having come to a stop on the trail there with us, his body continued moving and bouncing as if he were bounding down the mountain at high speed. When he saw me admiring his medicine gourd, he at once offered us the vessel, this being a well-documented sign of hospitable greeting in the Flower-Belt culture.

Robert did not reach for the gourd. He eyed past the scruffy man, up the path, toward the ancient tea tree gardens of Longshen. But the Flower-Belt fellow was quick to voice his displeasure:

"Stop!" he ordered, placing his hand in the air in front of Robert. "Drink from the gourd as a guest of the Flower-Belt people."

As you may remember, Robert Painter never drank alcohol. But as this was the mountain of the Flower-Belt people—and as we were guests in a foreign prefecture of a foreign land—even my friend Robert relented and took a healthy swig from the medicine gourd to stamp our entry. I took my medicine, too, before returning the medicine gourd to the strange, bouncing man.

Robert asked him: "What's your name?"

"Kang," said the man, dropping the sound back to us as he scampered up the dirt path ahead.

"Just Kang?" asked Robert.

"Kang is enough."

So we followed Kang.

The trail grew wider. Here and there, stilted wooden houses appeared among the trees. A series of red dirt paths converged with ours. Soon there were so many, it was impossible to tell which was which. This was it—Lotus Blossom Village—the home of the famous Longshen tea—a group of lonely, wooden houses perched atop the summit of Longshen Gorge.

Vines dangled passion fruits from the densely-foliated fruit trees. Other yet-unknown-to-me orange and red fruits dropped from their branches right before our eyes. Homely boys and girls ran about, chasing a bicycle tire they rolled beneath the stilted houses. "Try one," Kang suggested as he plucked one of the asymmetrical orange and red fruits and handed it to me.

Before I had a chance to try it, a striking, young girl emerged from one of the stilted houses nearby. She was dark and wild-eyed and walking right toward us. Robert and I stared unabashedly, our primal instincts primed from the physical exertion of our hike through the wood.

"Hey you!" She greeted us, unsure as to whether or not the two foreign *color wolves* could even understand. But when we reacted appropriately, she bade us to follow, which we, of course, did.

I had forgotten all about Kang until he released a loud and halting guffaw. He winced and contorted his face with jealousy, scorn and disappointment. Now that we were out of the wood, it was easy to see that Kang was dirty and swaying, with broken pieces of twig in his hair. So we ignored Kang and followed the girl, along the dirt paths to the top of the gorge. Hens with clutches of chicks scampered beneath every house. Human eyes, too, peered out to greet us from the dark, lofted entrances of the stilted houses.

"Two days from now is the summer moon," the girl told us, glancing back to make sure we could really understand. "There will be a festival."

We nodded eagerly and she smiled.

"This is my village. You will stay here."

十六

The mysterious girl led us to a stilted house on the far outskirts of the village. There she advised us to rest before she disappeared altogether.

The thick air inside the sparse hut was filled with the aroma of Tiger Balm and that peaty scent of sweating, ancient lumber. There were two bamboo cots and a woven bamboo floor mat. There was one electric lamp with no lampshade. A sack of sour, green passion fruits clung to a nail on the far wall. A pile of ripe melons rested in the corner.

It was evening now, and I was weary from the long hours we'd spent hiking in the jungle. Robert sat cross-legged on his cot, back erect, speaking the words of the Buddha, his body and his hempen shroud drenched in the fading light. He was jubilant, relaxed, and unconcerned about anything. He'd once spent a month meditating in India—not talking to anyone and eating only when they rang a bell—learning what he could from the Dharma masters. This, he told me, had altered his thinking permanently. We waited there in the cabin for a long time—reading, writing, and listening to soukous from Robert's pocket translating computer. Robert shared his poetry with me—mostly about love at first sight and the vastness of this ocean life—the *yin* and the *yang*—those contrasting forces which influence us all. I snacked on my mangoes and pears, and dug into the passion fruits from the nail on the far wall. The occasional gecko crawled the wall, stalking the flies that were attracted by the fresh fruit. Later, I left Robert and stepped outside. The sky was an impressionist oil painting, with all the colors—the blues, the pinks, the whites—all touched with a dusky shade of grey. Mosquitoes arose and the sun dipped into the jungle of night.

* * * * *

Of a sudden, the sound of men toasting over barbecue reverberated throughout the forest. Surprised, I retreated back inside the hut to query Robert, who was always far more knowledgeable in these matters than I. And in what was perhaps a vestigial display of English formality, Robert advised that we ought best wait for a proper invitation. This, as we knew it, consisted of a swig from somebody's medicine gourd. But to our lazy dismay that evening, our hosts never came, so we just lay in our cots listening, *just listening*, as the outside voices of the Flower-Belt elders carried far down into the valley.

* * * * *

When we awoke in the morning, there were chickens beneath our beds. I almost killed the head rooster, that cootling jackass bastard!

That night had been a deep sleep of infinite peace and relaxation, with no schedules or timetables. I felt the last bit of waste and excess from my life in America wash out, emulsifying the contrasting forces within, and joining them to the natural, luxurious beauty of my new surroundings. Well in line with these new feelings, Robert and I agreed to stage a visit to a famous tea temple rumored to be on the next mountain ridge over. We set out early, before anyone in the village had a chance to realize we were gone.

✸ ✸ ✸ ✸ ✸

As it turned out, the Temple of the Tea Deities wasn't just your run-of-the-mill Buddhist temple. It was a smattering of Burmese style mini-temples, all surrounded by an alpine meadow full of skinny cattle basking in the morning sunshine. Amid the cattle were a series of wooden, animist totems, popping up here and there at odd intervals between the cow pats. These totems pre-dated the Buddhist works by 800 to 1,000 years, Robert briefed me. Robert was sure it was these people—the ones who drove these totems into the ground all those years ago—who had planted the famous tea tree gardens of Longshen, the ones for which we had come from so far to find.

Despite the pedigree of their region's famous tea, the monks of this temple, like all monks from these parts, were young, ignorant farm boys wearing NBA basketball jerseys over their orange vestments. They were the second-born sons of second-born sons, and they mostly just ignored us while Robert meditated in the golden hall and I poked around the grounds, looking for interesting archeological artifacts.

After a time, I sauntered to the entrance of the temple, where a thousand-year-old tea tree grew from a terraced, garden staircase. There were chickens there too, and they gathered about me with their chicks, cooing lovingly. Soon Robert came out and put on his sandals. He flowed down the steps and under the arbor formed by the intertwined branches of the ancient tea tree. There he sat beside me and began to meditate.

十七

That afternoon, when we returned to the stockaded Flower-Belt village, there was a plume of ethereal, white smoke easing its way into the sky from the top of the gorge. It was in finding our way to the source of this alluring column of vapors, that Robert and I found our way to the most intriguing lodge.

A gangway beckoned us inward. We walked up the ramp and stooped beneath the sloping, wood-tiled roof. On the second floor, there was a large open-air balcony. Here, next to a wide doorway, a grey-haired woman tended to a few village-sized stew pots bubbling over a charcoal brazier. She stood there, solemnly stirring, watching. Then, when the time was right for us to enter, she nodded gently and stepped aside.

It was smoky past the ornate portière, and we could see the embers of a large, central fire pit below. All around us, cuts of meat were suspended to dry. Below—deep in the Flower-Belt hearth—I could make out the shapes of men's faces shuffling here and there in the darkness.

As we walked down, the smoke rose past us to meet the beams of light slipping in through the ancient roof. It was then when I could make out their features—the sharp eyebrows and big jowly smiles of the Flower-Belt elders, who bellowed great, big laughs from their brown, round bellies, then smiled and gave away their stools for Robert and me to sit.

Now Robert was completely in his element. Finally he was in a place where even his clothing fit. The Flower-Belt elders wore white, collarless jackets, unbuttoned in front as a matter of the fashion. These jackets were woven from hemp and the sleeves hung loosely, with silk ribbons of red and blue extended from each placket. Robert was jealous, of course, as he'd been trying to get his hands on one of these jackets from the dealers in Lime River for a long time, without any luck.

The Flower-Belt elders are famous for drinking copious amounts of their own, home-brewed rice wine. So we weren't at all surprised to find them heckling a few of the younger, warrior-types when we arrived. These younger fellows were impressive in appearance and in action. I, too, became impressed with several of the men who held large bamboo tubes between their thighs. They beat these tubes to create a tribal music that very much invigorated the others.

Robert and I did our best to introduce ourselves. The language of the Flower-Belt people was borne of the mountains and difficult to understand, but some of the younger members of the tribe spoke the Mandarin they had learned at the government school. Robert asked if there was a written form of their language. There wasn't and had never been. But the oral tradition, they told us, had been around since the flood of the creation story. The warrior-types then stood up in turns to each recite a piece of their origin. They beat their chests proudly as they passionately reenacted their favorite parts. It went something like:

There was a merciful goddess who rescued a boy and a girl during a terrible flood. This goddess was so merciful and benevolent that she plucked the two helpless children from the rough and rising waters at the head of the Yangzi, just when they may have otherwise drowned. On a drum fashioned from cattle hide, she floated them down the river to eventual safety on the Yangzi Plain.

Many years later, the same boy and girl returned to settle the gorge above the first turn in the river. They married, and became the first Flower-Belt family, generations of which sprang forth from their loins for centuries to come.

The Flower-Belt tribe prospered in the lowlands, tending to bunker crops of *Japonica* rice atop their water buffalo. The Flower-Belt chieftains were politically savvy too, and their nation came to dominate the other Tibeto-Burman-speaking groups living further into the Himalaya. This was, of course, until the Flower-Belts themselves were overtaken by the Duozu dynasty in the fourteenth century, A.D.

The young men demanded that Robert and me take more shots from their sling gourds. To encourage us, they grabbed ahold of their bamboo tubes and continued the pressing beat. So we obliged, taking hot slashes from their tippy gourds of fire water.

Then they asked us to explain the story of our ancestries, which we of course, weren't able to do in quite such a wonderful way. The Flower-Belt elders considered our inability to recite our origin tales utterly hilarious, and they forced us to apologize and take more shots of their strong alcohol as retribution.

＊ ＊ ＊ ＊ ＊

Now I don't consider myself an expert on the isolated, minority tribes of Yunnan—but I have been there with the Flower-Belt elders on top of Longshen Shan. I have seen their rituals, heard their guttural language, and drunk from the fire within their sling gourds. Yes, we were there in the muffled hushness of their inner sanctum, Robert and me, drinking and nodding in agreement even when we didn't understand—

—And, after a time, we all tramped back down the ramp of the long-house together, arm in arm, melodiously.

At this secluded spot of pure beauty, it was three-thousand meters down to the unnavigable Yangzi. The craggy rock faces on the other side of the gorge were separated from one another by dark scars of vast emptiness that flowed like cried tears into the valley below. I couldn't imagine anyone other than the Flower-Belt people ever getting used to this.

Because the next day was the Moon Festival—and we had been told this many times—no one was much in the mood for selling any tea. Instead, the large group of us, perhaps twelve in all, sat congregated beneath the tree which dangled bright red fruits with orange fluff and chiropteran wing petals. Vines of tiny watermelons wove around us in the underbrush. Everything here seemed alive and crawling in the humid dusk.

"Take this," said one of the men as he conked a watermelon open and threw half of it to me. The flesh inside was yellow and lush. As I ate, the water dripped down my wrists, almost to my elbows, before splashing to the ground.

* * * * *

Once our faces had grown hot and flushed from the drinking, Robert and I were taken back to our stilted hut—the one replete with the aroma of Tiger Balm and that humid scent of ancient lumber—where we were encouraged to fall asleep amid the sweet sounds of the virgin jungle.

十八

I opened my eyes to see Kang standing at the foot of the bed grinning, full of wonder, about to molest my left foot. This was altogether quite displeasing, and I was out of bed in a bleary-eyed instant, only half-jokingly taking a run at Kang, and when I did, he retreated to the doorway of the cabin, pointing, saying, "Outside, Outside."

I took my time getting dressed and drinking water that morning, and when I finally did meet Kang outside, he handed me over to the girl from the trail. She introduced herself as Li Mei, and her dark eyes at once scanned me in a way I didn't quite understand. It seemed like disgust, but it could have been fear as well.

In the gorge below, a sea of clouds stretched out like a canvas over all the Earth. Creamy dollops of white meringue fanned out into the valleys and everything below them ceased to exist—Song's plantations, the road back to civilization—all the way to Burma in one direction and Laos in the other.

Robert was sitting against the outside wall of our hut. His eyes were closed and he was meditating, legs crossed with a brown prayer shawl over his shoulders for warmth. His eyes opened on me, like the Buddha-sun rising. With a breath he took me in and then he took in the girl; with a second breath he took in the imbecile Kang and then exhaled.

Li Mei was our minder for this journey. She gestured for Kang to leave us, and, after an involuntary twitch of embarrassment, he did, but not before indicating to Li Mei that he planned to complain about it to Lao Song later.

Naturally, when Li Mei invited Robert and me to buy a quantity of first-flush, autumn tea we gleefully accepted. Li Mei nodded and scampered off down the trail and into the trees ahead. Robert and I were quick to follow, with Robert bounding and free-flowing, ready to do business in the funny sort of way that only a Buddhist can.

I took this opportunity on the trail to try to learn a little more about Li Mei. She was bouncing in all the right ways as she moved, and I couldn't help but to notice. As soon as Robert was distracted by the first tea bushes lining the path, I scooted behind her to ask, "So how come it's you taking us to see the tea and not Lao Song or the elders?"

Li Mei didn't look at me. She stared only at the trail ahead:

"I am the prettiest. Song thought you would like me the best."

* * * * *

The tea factory was nothing more than a rough patch of dirt cut into the side of the mountain—a plot of weedy, rugged terrain. When we arrived, there were knee-high heaps of tea lying all around. This tea was fresh; it looked as if it had been rolled and fried that very morning. The tea trees themselves were nearby, too, scattered about the forest surrounding the property.

"Not very well looked after in this area, are they?" Robert suggested. "Three, *hmm*, maybe four meters tall," he measured, eyeing an especially interesting copse of thin, gnarly tea tree trunks. "Quite old, I would say—at least a couple hundred years, and probably a few here that are substantially older." Robert pinched a tea leaf from one of the drying racks and examined the botanical structure. Then he rolled a few leaves between his fingers and inhaled their delicate aroma. "When was this picked?" He asked Li Mei.

"Yesterday evening. It's the first flush of this year's autumn tea."

"Ah, but this tea looks like it's lost too much humidity already from the rolling and frying," Robert negotiated, smiling his broad Englishman's smile. "We are here at the behest of Lao Pu, and Lao Pu only drinks spring tea," Robert announced, still negotiating to show he knew what was what when it came to tea. Then suddenly he paused for a moment, thinking aloud to himself. "What was the rainfall like last year where this was grown, anyway?"

To this Li Mei was dour and unaccommodating. "This is Flower-Belt Longshen tea," she spat back as she picked a leaf from the largest of piles. "Last autumn, a businessman from Taiwan came and bought the entire mountain's worth of autumn tea in just one day." She posed with her hand on her hip before adding: "Autumn tea was good enough for him. He'll probably come back and buy it all again this year. Maybe I should just save it—"

"Can we just try the tea?" I interjected to ask, parched and hungry for caffeine, thinking I was probably doing us all a favor. Li Mei nodded and beckoned to the storehouse, where a boy of ten or eleven came out to greet us from the darkness. He brought with him a large, black kettle, and placed it on the mud-brick range used for frying the tea. Robert pulled three clay teacups from his hempen purse, giddy with anticipation. Once the water was hot, Li Mei worked the range with a porcelain bowl, pouring the tea water many times over, first to wash the leaves, then to present our long-anticipated first tastes. Bits and pieces of charcoal from the fire flew into, and then back out of our cups. The young boy offered me a cigarette, and I accepted, despite the fact I had already quit. It didn't matter. I washed it all down with the fruity broth of Pu'er, waiting eagerly for Li Mei to pour every next taste.

Robert, too, was impressed.

"How much did the Taiwanese pay?" he asked.

Li Mei looked up from the fire: "1,000 *kuai* per kilogram."

"Our price should be lower," suggested Robert. "Since we are locals." Then he winked at me.

Li Mei scanned the racks of tea, counting and calculating with her head cocked to the side and her eyes busily engaged in math.

十九

When we returned to Lotus Blossom Village, there was excitement in the air. The music was gearing up for the festival, and we danced around gaily with our satchels filled to bursting with tea. Robert and I had the first installment—whatever we could grab in loose tea. We'd return the next day with Li Mei to pick up the rest, once it had been appropriately pressed into six *tong* worth of cakes. Everything had been a success and now there was going to be a party, and I couldn't help but to be taken up in all the hubbub.

Squat, little tables were placed along the dusty trails between the houses; hens and cocks with opaline plumage scurried about here and there—all manner of fowl seemingly unaware that the old women of the village were plotting bowls for them of various shapes and sizes and depths. The old women argued over which bowls should go where, and whose dishes would turn out to be the most delicious. They wondered aloud if this dish needed more salt or if that dish had too much already. These were those fine, broad-shouldered women with that long and luxuriant

Flower-Belt hair. Some even wore in their hair the flowers from the melon trellises, whose vines tumbled about helter-skelter at our feet.

I sat down on a stool at one of the little tables and waited, and it wasn't long before one of the women appeared with a bowl of Yunnan's famous *Cross Bridge* noodles, the freshest rice noodles garnished with the most savory of flavors: stone-ground chili, minced garlic, chopped cilantro and freshly-roasted peanuts—all bathed in soy sauce and sprinkled with white sugar. And on top of all that there were even two hard-boiled quail eggs and a puff of white fungus. *Eat that if you're a pro, boy*! And I ate it down gleefully, working my way through the noodles with firm chopstick movements, tipping the bowl to drink the red broth as they've done here for generations.

Just then, there was a great commotion as the Flower-Belt elders paraded into the village from one of the trails coming down the mountain. The men marched into the center of town in formations of threes and fours, banging on their bamboo pipes and hooting and hollering and singing victoriously. Some were holding bewildered chickens beneath their arms. Some held aloft bottles of *baijiu* or cakes of tea. Others squeezed and massaged the bleeding organs of a freshly-slaughtered bull. The younger warriors hoisted rodents on spears, proudly displaying the spoils of their Flower-Belt marksmanship. Women joined too, holding eggs or wine, or luscious papayas from the gardens. Greater and greater numbers of Flower-Belt villagers came out from their stilted houses to join the parade, and each one added to the shrieks and hollers of delight.

The brown bellies of the barrel-chested men shone out from between the lapels of their white, Flower-Belt coats as they worked together to carry a ceremonial drum out of the lodge. One of the largest of the men, a warrior with a broad forehead and a beautifully flowing mane of hair, hoisted the gigantic instrument into the air above his head. This feat prompted nothing short of cheers and cries of amazement from the gathering crowd.

The face of the drum was painted with the orange Flower-Belt sun—its nine sun-spokes radiating out to greet the world below in every direction. The oldest of the Flower-Belt elders approached and caressed the image, playing to the crowd's excitement. Once this elder had determined the amount of deference displayed by the crowd was indeed the appropriate amount, he bade the deliverers of the drum to place it onto a ceremonial stand. With this act complete, the crowd grew tense and silent in anticipation.

"This drum is the drum of our ancestors!" The old man spoke.

As he did, he was at once met with great positivity from the crowd.

"…During their time, too, they beat the cadence of this drum…"

The crowd cheered so loudly, I was sure the people at the Tourist Bureau in Pomasha could hear.

Satisfied, the old man continued:

"Now that your ancestors have ceased to exist here on this Earth, they have become the Earth itself and bestow unto us this drum, the symbol of our people, the Flower-Belt tribe.

"Each of them we have lost," the elder continued as he scanned the crowd before pointing to a large woman in the front row:

"You! Your great uncle—"

He scanned again and found a child holding a piece of candy:

"Your grandmother, too—"

He pointed to a somber man in the back of the crowd:

"Your wife, old friend—"

And despite the intense anticipation these words prompted within the seething crowd, the elder grew quiet and turned again to the drum to gently pat its face:

"They are all here, inside."

Then he slapped the portrait of the sun on the rough hide and cackled with vigor:

"And today, as we do every year when the largest moon of the summer rises above our home in the gorge of the Longshen forest, we wake our ancestors with song and ask them once again for their blessings!"

The great patriarch, now shaking with age and emotion, took hold of a sling gourd brought to him by the warriors. This particular decorative vessel was five or six times the size of any other medicine gourd in the village. It was so big, in fact, it took several strong men to lift it to the old man's mouth for a ceremonial libation.

* * * * *

We sat around the fire ring drinking and singing that night; it didn't matter that I didn't know the songs or the words. By this time, as far as I was concerned, I was and had always been Flower-Belt people. We shared the same collective unconscious, after all, and like leaves on a tree, we would all return to become our piece of the Earth once more. The animist totems on the next ridge over were there for me to discover, just as they had been for the Buddhist monks who took control of the temple, and for the Flower-Belt tribe who was in control before that. I could understand everyone, I thought, just by looking at them and *feeling*. Mostly what I understood was that these Flower-Belt guys wanted to see how much I could drink. For my own part, I wanted to play the bamboo pipe and make music. One of the warriors said I could try, but only if I'd agree to drink a bowl of beer with him first. So I obliged and grabbed the bamboo pipe from between his legs as we all sang together in cadence. We pleaded our calls again and again as if we were trying to wake the Gods.

* * * * *

At midnight, squeals began to ring out from the backhouses surrounding the village. It started slowly, but rang out sure and true at measured intervals underneath our tribal beats. It seemed everyone, everywhere was slaughtering and butchering hogs. In went offerings of oranges and incense and cigarettes and out came tubs of white lard and porcine rib cages, then huge, pork hindquarters meant for hanging and smoking.

A fierce warrior called to me as I drifted besottedly between the stilted houses under the pale moonlight. He explained quite excitedly about a hog being butchered on the path near the center of the village. It was his family's hog, and was by far the largest in the village. He needed a few strong men to help lift the animal onto a table for immediate slaughter.

The warrior led me to the site of the execution, where we all took our places around the 500-pound hog. I helped to lift and pin the heaving animal as it fought us off with fits and squirms.

Once we had secured the legs, a man with peafowl plumage tucked into the lapel of his communist-style military jacket approached. He smiled broadly, then nonchalantly slit the beast's throat with a long, sharp knife. The life drained quickly from behind the animal's dark eyes. As it did, the old women of the village clamored around to catch bowlfuls of the gushing arterial blood. The men drank the raw blood from the bowls, cheersing merrily and swallowing it down in big globfuls. "Drink this," ordered the man in the military jacket.

"Here, drink this instead," Li Mei appeared among the revelers, wearing full Flower-Belt regalia and a silver ornamental headband. She handed me a small gourd filled with thick *baijiu*.

The girl was radiant there and then, and it was my delusion to think I was seeing the Iron Goddess of Mercy herself, like the sun and the stars and the moon above. That night was the night of the moon festival alright, and I was there—where the alchemy of the moon and the blood and the *baijiu* sent us spinning, dancing like primal animals under the celestial light.

二十

At the time, I knew nothing at all, and even now I admit I'll probably never get all the way down to the bottom of things. But as I awoke in the darkness of that thatch hut in Lotus Blossom Village, I knew it instantly. The event I had heard so much about since arriving in China, the one that makes fear the distinguishing characteristic of all mainland Chinese—*the one mistake that ruins your life*—it had happened to me, just as it happens to everyone eventually in China. Li Mei was not asleep. She lay there next to me on the bed, wearing nothing but a black t-shirt. When the girl noticed I was awake, she dressed herself and left promptly.

I turned away from the door, feeling unsure and vulnerable. I wasn't sure what to do, and something didn't quite feel right. If things went sour, I had only the Buddhist, Robert, as a wing-man, and it might be hard to convince him to fight, especially over a girl. It took me a long time to rouse myself that morning, but once I had, I ventured out to look for the water kettle.

I found Robert immediately. He was meditating in his brown prayer shawl, his back erect against the outside wall of our stilted, thatch hut. I took special note of Robert that morning. It was unusual for him to be muttering as he sat—this being that he was so practiced in meditation. I took this strange omen to mean I should leave Robert there to his own business. But when I tried to pass, he trapped me there with his steely, wild eyes:

"You think you can sneak around me that easily, Small Tiger—or whatever cute name it is you have picked out for yourself?"

I was taken aback.

"Where are you going?" He asked me in a booming voice. I could tell by the seriousness in his eyes that he thought he already knew the answer.

"To get some water."

"To get some water?" Robert repeated after me, disbelievingly.

"Uh-huh."

"And to look for Li Mei?"

I was quite taken aback.

"Sure," I answered: "It's possible."

"Why?" Robert asked rather petulantly. Especially, I thought, for a man who was so pious and sure of himself.

"No reason," I answered, "What's going on with the tea?"

Robert ignored my proposition for a change of topic, and instead demanded, in a surly sort of way:

"Did it ever occur to you that I might have wanted to take her to see a movie?"

I was confused, to say the least, and this much must have shown plainly across my face, because Robert then explained:

"She told me last night she'd never been to a movie theater." He shook his head with a look of contempt. "I bet you didn't even know that."

"I'm sorry Robert. I didn't know you'd be into that sort of thing."

Robert was a straight-up Buddhist monk, and at least sometimes, he really believed he was well on the road to enlightenment. But he was a man, too, and, after all, all men need sex.

"To be honest Robert, I hadn't considered this. That's your business—what you want with her—I would only assume that you would just go for it. That's how it works."

"You Americans are all the same. You don't give a damn about anyone other than yourselves. You haven't been in Asia long enough to understand discretion."

Robert cocked his head in an arrogant sort of way before looking to me with a disdainful smirk, "You may need to learn a little discretion now, Small Tiger, and fast. I don't think anyone told you yet—or maybe they did and you just didn't listen—but the girl you slept with last night is also the girl engaged to marry Lao Song!"

✳ ✳ ✳ ✳ ✳

That afternoon the sexual pressures of Lotus Blossom Village continued to take their toll on Robert's and my union. Despite what Robert had disclosed to me about her betrothal, I couldn't stop thinking about Li Mei. The tiny, thatch hut still smelt of melons and sex, and no amount of exotic, local fruit carried in from outside could change anything about that now.

Robert and I went about hedging our libidos in our own ways. Robert practiced Tai chi in the garden and upped his medication schedule. I took to the washroom for a cold shower. To my pleasure and disappointment, I chose a time when Li Mei had just finished and the air was still redolent with her scent. It was maddening. And I thought:

Robert has feelings for the girl. This much is certain. And this is the first time I am ever seeing feelings like this out of him—whatever that means. He planned to work her over—oh, yes, he did—even if he was going to do it in his own peculiar, Buddhist sort of way.

What the hell am I gonna do with a girl from Lotus Blossom Village, anyway? I was competitive, to be sure, but not to the point of forfeiting the common good. From what little I knew of Li Mei, I sensed she was trying to seek out a better life for herself, probably somewhere far away from Lotus Blossom Village. I wanted more of Li Mei to be certain, and I couldn't help but think she wanted something more from me—but now there was Robert and his sudden, sexual awakening. I wasn't at all sure what to do.

"Let's go pick up the rest of your tea," Li Mei suggested, flicking her wrist in the general direction of the trail that led between the mountain ridges to the tea factory.

Robert and I agreed and followed, despite the tension that was still very much between us. We walked in a line—Li Mei first, then Robert, then me, all tramping down the familiar trail, through the vines and the greenery and the mysterious underbrush. Our pace was brisk and it was surprising how quickly we arrived given the lengthy distance.

At the tea factory, I immediately took to helping Li Mei unload the tea cakes from the now-dismantled pressing and drying platforms. Robert craned his neck over my shoulder to get a better view of the tea cakes, and of Li Mei.

"Fifteen kilograms?" He asked.

"This is five *tong*," Li Mei said decisively. "We had only enough this flush to make five *tong* plus these two extra cakes." She pulled two, loose tea cakes back out of the rice sacks I had helped her to pack and presented them to us for inspection.

"So in that case, you'll need to give me back some of the money I gave you," said Robert. "Because didn't we give you enough money for six full *tong*?"

Li Mei nodded in agreement, "Yes. Your money is at the hotel down the path. We can finish our business there."

* * * * *

We followed the trail down the mountain in a different direction, all in a straight line, nobody talking. In several long minutes—or so it seemed—we were out of the jungle and into the foothills, where everything turned to dust. The trail widened here; tire tracks from four wheel drive vehicles cut into the fine sand of the road. We were grateful then, because the town of Pomasha was suddenly near and visible, and we had but a banana grove yet to traverse. I noticed now how thirsty I had become from the journey down the mountain. Robert the Buddhist had become thirsty too, and he said as much, which was a rarity for him.

Luckily the girl led us into the first building on the edge of town. It was an unimposing structure with a marquee that read: *The Pretty Baby Hotel*. Once we were inside, it took my eyes some time to adjust. One thing was certain; the familiar and discordant sounds of karaoke wafted from down the hallway.

We followed Li Mei into one of the rooms. It was a sparse room with a twin bed covered in simple padding. In one corner, there was a wardrobe with a broken door. In another, there was an old, heavy television atop a dusty TV stand. Posters of K-Pop heartthrobs hung to the white-lime walls all around.

"This is my room," explained Li Mei proudly.

Robert and I must have appeared puzzled, because she continued, "I am Flower-Belt people but I also live here sometimes."

Li Mei picked up the television remote from the bed and gazed around the room in a self-satisfied fashion. "I don't even pay rent here. I work a few afternoons a week in the hotel, whenever they need me—and they let me stay in this room and keep my things. Here is pretty good. Here has hot water and television and young people. When I work here, I can buy the things I want to buy. Not like a stupid village girl on the mountain." She nodded to a dresser in the corner of the room, upon which sat a collection of knock-off handbags and shiny knick-knacks and cheap jewelry. This modest assortment of goods was as intricately displayed as if it were a part of a famous museum collection. Li Mei sat down in front of us on the bed and admired the things lovingly.

Then there was a knock at the door, and I was displeased to see Kang peek his tousled head out into the room. No one asked him to leave, so he lingered there, giggling stupidly to himself as we conducted our bit of tea business with Li Mei.

Soon after the money had been exchanged, Kang began to act up. He demanded, in his own peculiar sort of way, that Robert and I accompany him to sing a few songs down the hall. In keeping with the spirit of the good relations we thought it might afford us, Robert and I agreed, and each took a long swig from the medicine gourd we were offered. We then followed Kang down the hallway, toward the intoxicating music.

* * * * *

In any karaoke (or KTV) parlor in China, you will first be led into a private room. Inside, there is a faux-leather sectional; a flat screen TV; and a coffee table with beer, wine, sunflower seeds, and other sundries. Another thing to remember is that in any KTV crowd anywhere in China, there's always a Chinese guy who speaks a little English. Even in Pomasha at the end of the world, there was still one guy who could speak a little English. In Pomasha, his name was Skill.

Skill wore a long-sleeve, buttoned-down shirt and he had a full and weighty keychain latched to his belt loop with a carabineer. He was a Pomasha local for sure, truculent and scrappy. After a haughty greeting, he seated himself at the dais in the center of the dimly-lit room. Here he fumbled about the list of songs displayed on the console like someone who knew what he was doing.

"Do you want to sing?" Skill asked me, not making eye contact, still working his way through the list of songs. There was a cordless microphone on the table. Skill picked it up and waved it in my direction, as one might do in teasing a dog with a biscuit.

I shook my head indecisively.

Robert had gone to buy the beer, and, after a few more morsels of my awkward conversation with Skill, Robert returned, followed by three servers and Kang. The servers brought with them a case of warmish beer, a bottle of red wine, a vase full of ice, and a collection of shot glasses.

We did the manly thing and started drinking and carousing, in spite of the tension everyone still felt in the room. But, as is often the case when alcohol is being consumed, soon everything was forgotten, and every one of us, even Robert, who was drinking only as necessary, was feeling good and singing. Skill started us off with the obligatory, one-man rendition of Celine Dion's *My Heart Will Go On*. For an encore, he did Elton John's *Can*

You Feel the Love Tonight. He used the time between songs to cater to the audience, proudly explaining how he had used these songs to improve his mastery of the English language.

All this singing took what felt like a long time. The room was dark and Robert and I took turns throwing fresh grapes from the fruit plate at Kang while Skill continued his performance.

The next thing that happened was something I'd heard legends about. It was the kind of thing that men, young and old, talk about in locker rooms and at barber shops when their women aren't around. It's the kind of thing that everyone in China knew to be true, but that a young man from Columbus, Ohio, couldn't dream of until he saw it for himself.

A seductive, high-hipped hostess in a gold and black vest sashayed into the room. She was followed by a whole line of girls, serried for inspection. They ranged from too young in age to about thirty. It was an impressive collection for such a small town. There were a few thick girls from the Pomasha countryside. There were also a few tall Mongolians. There were some fresh and tender young things, made up to look like Japanese schoolgirls. They were disinterested and aloof and mostly just dawdled about, checking their electronic devices. Then there were the veterans, long-haired and well put-together. They yelped with surprise when they laid eyes on the strange, rich foreigners. The boldest among them crammed their bodies into the center of the room to make themselves more visible. They clawed at the air and turned at the angles they knew, from years of plying this trade under these conditions, would display the best of their features.

At once I felt the intense fire that had been lit within Robert's being, Buddhism be damned! I watched him exhale and breathe in the girls. I watched him rub his red mustaches and goatee, unable to keep me and the rest of the world from knowing what was going on inside his head as he watched these writhing women move—and finally I understood just why Robert Painter needed to be a Buddhist. At that thought—as if he knew exactly what I was thinking—Robert sprung up with a start and bounded out of the room. I remained there and examined the impressive phalanx of girls, not at all sure what to do.

Some of the veterans started grabbing for the beer and wine. Behind them, the schoolgirls in the tall socks punched away at their phones next to the line of tall Mongolians, who looked uncertain as to where they even were. The scene grew raucous, and the room was soon thickly spread with many competing and pungent aromas. One of the professionals sat on the sofa next to me and began to rub my thigh.

"How does this work?" I asked, in English.

She just nodded.

"We don't have this in Ohio," I protested weakly. But soon enough, as could happen to anyone, I just started nodding yes to everything.

二十二

When Lao Song showed up at the Pretty Baby Hotel, I was probably too drunk. We had made the switch from beer to *baijiu*, which is never a good switch to make in rural China in the early afternoon.

Kang and Skill stood with deference to Lao Song, the rubber baron and the owner of the Pretty Baby Hotel—but I didn't—choosing instead to slink down into the polyurethane sofa and hide. I sipped silently on warm beer, and after their cigarettes were distributed and lit, I heard Song ask his dogsbodies about the *laowai*. None of them could really tell the difference between Robert and me, but Song was certain that some *laowai* had sullied his name. A pang of fear hit my heart and I expected the worst as the men marched down the hallway to find Robert. For a moment, I marveled at how quickly things could change, and I fantasized that everything would be ok, and that Lao Song and his posse would still be in the mood for drinking and conversation once this ugliness was over—but as I followed them to the familiar room down the hall, I realized the situation had developed far past the point of discussion.

A bewildered Robert was sitting shirtless in his hempen trousers at the foot of Li Mei's bed. Lao Song was pointing angrily at Li Mei, ignoring Robert, focusing instead, all of his intense rage unto the girl. The dastardly henchman, Skill, grabbed Li Mei from the bed by her long and lustrous Flower-Belt hair and dragged the screaming girl across the floor toward Lao Song. Song cocked his hand as far back as he could and released, channeling all of his anger unmercifully across Li Mei's jaw.

Of a sudden, Robert was nothing like a serene and contemplative bodhisattva. He looked like Sun Wukong right there and then, and I never saw a man move in the way that Robert did in that moment. Like a swaying mantis, he sprung toward Lao Song—right across the concrete floor of that spartan room in the Pretty Baby Hotel. He was there intercepted by Kang, who had himself produced a small but sharp dagger from his trousers-pocket.

Robert, the Buddhist, lunged to meet his foe as Kang waved the knife between them for all to see, still grinning and giggling despite the seriousness of the situation. I felt like I was watching this situation unfold from eight-thousand miles away. *How did I get here?* I had no role to play in this strange drama on the edge of the world. Robert, a meter or two away, felt differently. With a modified Tai chi movement, fluid and graceful, he disarmed a stupefied Kang. In that same movement, he flipped the sharp weapon into his own firm hand.

What happened next was over in a flash, but to this day, it replays effortlessly in my mind, click by click, so that every motion is clear and eternal. Robert, his eyes focused, his arm extended, drove the knife into

Kang's abdomen, releasing a perceptible amount of Kang's life with each thrust, like puffs of steam spilling forth from an overboiling tea kettle.

Kang cowered and grabbed at his abdomen and fell back into Li Mei's bed. Robert stood above his vanquished adversary, the blood from his knife dripping down onto the floor from his wrist like the sweetest of watermelon. No one else in the room moved. The others stood watching in disbelief, just as I did. Kang writhed on the bed, struggling, clutching his wounds as the blood pooled under the small of his back on the mattress.

Skill was holding Li Mei by her hair, and he used it to jerk the cowering girl down to the ground. "Do you see what you've done?" He cried as he elbowed the girl's skull into the cement floor.

Li Mei shrieked in pain.

"Do you see what you've done in Lao Song's hotel?" Skill demanded an answer, but the girl just cried more and more loudly.

As I watched Kang gulp for air, the color escaped from his face. Shock set in. He jerked into strange contortions on the bed as the dark pool of blood gathering below his midsection began to drip through the mattress and onto the floor. Kang was staring right at me when he died. He seemed to me to be in a distant place. How strange this must have been for him to die staring at me, a foreigner. I was probably the first he had ever seen or met, and then—

Robert leapt across the room toward Skill and Lao Song. Skill dropped Li Mei and she crumbled to the floor, weeping. Robert briefly halted his progress toward the men, allowing the girl, who was shaking violently, some time to clear out before more of the badness that was to come.

* * * * *

The impulse to flee came suddenly, once Robert was through with his act of vengeance. I ran out of lobby of the Pretty Baby Hotel as quickly as I could and jumped onto the first motorcycle taxi in line at the curb.

"Take me to the closest bus station with a bus to Lime River," I demanded of the startled driver.

"That's all the way in Pingxing," he protested.

"Yes! Go!" I shouted.

The *moto* man just sat there dumbly, so I opened my mouth and whispered the magic words:

"I will pay you one-hundred *kuai*."

The driver kick-started the bike and I was gone.

二十三

The bus from Pingxing was not an express bus. It stopped at every town and city along the Pan-Asian Expressway, picking up rag-tag people and dropping them off further on down the road. The aisles of bunks inside in the bus were rank with the sour smell of dirty, sleeping humans. Unwashed linens, ragged metal edges, that awful smell, and *Lo!* quite by chance, the back seat open with that one, lonesome, life-giving window, ripe with all the fresh air in Yunnan.

The atmosphere outside was thick with time fog. I nudged the window open to try to relax. But it took me a while to calm down. If someone had to use the bathroom, the driver stopped the bus. If someone wanted to buy a bag of chopped green mango on the side of the road, the driver stopped the bus. It was slow going, and this was altogether agitating since I was on the run.

We wound around, and down the mountains. The whole time I worried and wondered: *What is my role here in this strange turn of events?* This, despite the fact that I kept telling myself: *laowai* in China are only ever on their own, and in the final analysis I needed only to look out for myself. Down. Down. Down. Through the tunnels of Yunnan. Moles we were. Twisting, turning, scurrying moles. Everyone hiding something, some more than others.

It must have been some horrible psychological reaction to the event I'd witnessed, but I felt eerily distant. I reveled in the motion of the bus ride that day. I couldn't help but to appreciate the beauty of life, and the adventure I'd found. *And, Kang?* Well, there probably wasn't any need to worry about that. The authorities, made up of committees and committees of men like Eight Fortunes Liu, would never care about someone as unimportant as that.

We travelled down the mountains, until papaya trees popped up like funny little moonmen through the fog. And I realized it was a selfish thing to do in the first place, to come to China—and it occurred to me that leaving Robert in Pomasha the way that I had might just be in keeping with my character. Yet as the lurching bus made its way along the dragon spine of Yunnan, I grasped my backpack, and in it, a small amount of the tea which had been our mission. Fragrant notes of camphor and apricot poured out of the bag to fill the heavy air in the back of the bus. I knew I needed to get this special tea to Lao Pu, no matter how small the quantity. I didn't know what to say about Robert, but I hoped desperately that getting the magic tea to Lao Pu might provide a measure of redemption against my selfish nature.

* * * * *

I didn't see anyone from the tea shop for several weeks. In the days after I returned to Lime River from Pomasha, Robert didn't show and Lai Sao was probably still busy tending to Lao Pu in the hospital.

Breaking the news about Robert to Lao Pu and Lai Sao wasn't something I was ready to do—so I decided to get out of town. I could never be a part of anything real in China anyway. A foreigner could leave and never come back and no one would ever be surprised. I wanted to remember how far away Lime River was from everything. I wanted to go as far away as I could without running away entirely. I needed to go somewhere where I could feel small again.

Before I left, I stopped at the tea shop and dropped a burlap satchel on the stoop at the entrance. I stuck a note to it which read, roughly, in Chinese:

> *Lai Sao,*
>
> *This is a small sack of tea from Longshen Mountain, Lotus Blossom Village. It's a gift from Robert to Lao Pu. He hopes it helps and wishes Lao Pu a speedy recovery. Sorry there isn't more. Wishing you both the best,*
>
> *Small Tiger*

二十四

Lincoln Jones was the American student who had first introduced me to Robert. The three of us made fast friends in Lime River in the mid 2000s, with me and Lincoln mostly scheming about how to pick up girls, while Robert hung around doing the Robert sorts of things he used to do. And I distinctly remember Lincoln advising me to give Robert a chance, when, freshly arrived from Ohio, I briefly considered Robert altogether too foreign and strange to get to know in the way that later, of course, I did.

But not too long after my arrival in Yunnan, young Lincoln grew tired of Lime River, and of Kunming, and eventually of western China altogether. He craved more action and, to put it crassly, new women. So he did a brief stint in Hunan, the birthplace of Chairman Mao, then moved on up the line to live in fashionable, hip, and trendy Beijing.

At the time of my visit, Lincoln had fallen in with a group of American expatriates who were hanging out a lot in the Wudaokou district. Lincoln's friends were all pretending to study Mandarin at Beijing's finest universities. I say pretending because mostly they were just hiding out from their parents, screwing the locals and screwing each other, smoking cheap cigarettes and drinking even cheaper alcohol. Most of them couldn't speak Chinese for shit and cared even less about the culture. This excluded my friend, Lincoln of course, who, owing to his many years immersed in the badlands of Yunnan, was the real deal.

As a rule, Lincoln didn't speak much and when he did, he did so softly, tenderly, as if he was never quite confident in what he was saying. Despite these outward appearances, he told me how he had recently been successful in taking home his first international runway model, a badge of honor among his particular circle of friends. Of this he was immensely proud.

* * * * *

On my first day in Beijing, Lincoln took me to see the Forbidden City, a palace complex separated from the rest of Central Beijing by a 26-foot-high protective wall. At one point in the distant past, the Forbidden City, now a marvel of a dynastic museum, was considered to be the foothold of Heaven's supreme power on Earth. This claim was substantiated by the dominance of the emperor: his armies, his slaves, his concubines, his ability to build high walls. Throughout the Ming and Qing dynasties, the Chinese instituted harmony through supremacy, like all great nation-states—from the Flower-Belts to the Americans—have endeavored to do. I couldn't help but to wonder when the tide might turn back to Beijing, and what this change might mean for the rest of us.

Lincoln was a gourmand who shared my love of the wild and wonderful taste adventure that is China. He took me on a tour of all his favorite restaurants and watering holes in Wudaokou. In trendy student bars, we danced with his expatriate circle of friends until early in the morning, until Lincoln's long, black hair dangled wet into his eyes, matted and dripping. Lincoln had the face of a cherub, with white skin and the natural rouge of youth on his cheeks. What was most amazing to me, was that what Lincoln had said was true. We *did* go out with that season's crop of runway models stationed in Beijing. In fact, it seemed like we went out with all of them.

Lincoln had not, as he had intended, continued his study in Beijing. He, like me, had found a much more lucrative way to earn a living. His profession combined his knowledge of the rough lands and people of Yunnan with his new position at the social center of the Sino-expatriate network. This work, more or less, involved making two trips per year back to the comparatively lawless areas of Yunnan near the Burmese border. There, Lincoln would acquire large quantities of purple-tipped cannabis from one particular minority connection at a pittance. He then smuggled each shipment by train from Kunming back to Beijing, disguising his shipment in elaborate Pu'er tea gift boxes. This was usually about forty kilograms per trip, in case you'd be interested to know.

In Beijing, Lincoln sold the pot at a nine thousand percent mark-up to extravagant foreign expatriates, all of whom were afraid of being cheated by the local Chinese dealers, who themselves would prefer not to be dealing with dumbass foreigners anyway. So everyone won, which, according to the rules of *guanxi,* was an important consideration.

Lincoln was cool. He lived, fittingly, downtown, in a post-modern high-rise apartment in the trendiest part of Beijing. He had a view of the newly completed CCTV Tower—*the Doughnut*—a wonder of modern architecture that had been completed only a year or two before. The convenient location made for quick excursions to and from scenic spots within the heart of the ancient capital via the ultra-modern and ultra-fast subway system. Many of Lincoln's high-rise neighbors were the kept women of successful Asian businessmen, the kind of businessmen who drift around the globe and stop into their cities only every-so-often at odd hours. For this reason, among others, frequent comings and goings were not out of place—even late at night—and Lincoln and my excursions—as well as his secret business dealings—remained brisk and undetected by any authorities who might care to bother.

During the last few days of my stay, we finished out the tourist route. Lincoln was a gracious host. He even brought me to a secret, sparsely visited section of the Great Wall. I am therefore one of only a small percentage of visitors, Chinese or foreign, to have walked along this famous site in solitude. Lincoln didn't even bother to come, for by this time he was a trifle bored with the Wall. He preferred instead to sit in the shade against the base of the massive structure, drinking from a flask of whisky. That day it was hot and clear at the top, and I was glad to be alone, gazing out along the endless edifice to either side. I was at peace and nothing could shake me from it. It was unusual how still I became, despite everything I was trying to forget about in Yunnan.

It must also be said that we two Americans did a fair amount of shopping in Houhai and Xidan. This seemed to really perk Lincoln up, as he had money to spend. We bought fake movie star sunglasses and novelty t-shirts and imported books. Lincoln also bought brand-name perfumes and makeup items, which he said were to be made as gifts to girls. And—as I may have already mentioned—we did an enormous amount of international dining. We ate Korean hot pot, German sauerbraten and sausages, perfectly-roasted Xinjiang lamb, Hungarian goulash, good old American pancakes with tons of maple syrup, Dairy Queen sundaes, barbecue ribs, Peking duck, and beef hamburgers. I was so happy at the sight of all this food after being in Yunnan for so long that I cried, hiding my embarrassing tears as I gushed about how these exotic meals alone would have been enough to make the trip. And, for a moment, I considered just staying. But I was running out of money with Lincoln in Wudaokou, so when it came time for him to make his presentations to the next round of international runway models, I left Beijing and its trendy student bars and returned to my austere, tea-drinking life in Lime River.

二十五

Back in Lime River, I spent as much time on my own as I could, doing my adventure thing. Mostly I was just avoiding anyone who might ask me something about Robert. Fortunately for me, this was easier than it normally might have been. By this point in summer, most of the Lime River locals chose to stay indoors until evening, when the oppressive heat of day had somewhat subsided. During these quiet afternoons and sometimes early evenings, most of my wanderlust trails ended on the banks of the Mekong, where I'd skip rocks and take off my shirt to admire my brown body in the tropical sunlight.

Then one late afternoon, when the water was too low to skip stones, I stopped in at Robert's house—the one nestled in the grove of banana and *Ficus* trees under the impressive spans of the New Bridge. To my disappointment but not my surprise, Robert still wasn't there.

On my way home, after I'd strolled the broad avenue lined with the yellow-flowering trees and passed the Drum Tower, I saw a welcome sight. The door to Pursuing Pure Perfection was propped open in a familiar way.

I was excited, but also a little hesitant. Now must be the time to tell Lao Pu or Lai Sao about Robert, I reasoned. I'd waited long enough. So in spite of any remaining trepidation, I stepped inside the shop and made my way into the back of the tasting room.

And wouldn't you know it? Robert was there, sitting behind the camphor-laurel trunk. The man himself was entirely surrounded: towering stacks of tea cakes wrapped in bamboo paper teetered all around his bony body.

* * * * *

At first I felt only the uncomfortable sensation of sharing the tasting room with someone I had watched kill a man not a month prior. Robert's reason for stabbing the idiot Kang was a just one, but even the evidence of this truth in my memory couldn't prevent the four walls of the tasting room from closing in all around. I had no idea how killing would change a man, either instantly, or slowly, over time. I was worried we would have to start all over, Robert and me. I had so many questions and I wasn't at all sure where to begin.

I was relieved to discover the discomfort was mutual; Robert and I worked our way through several pots of tea in abject silence. Robert was taking quiet notes on all the subtle flavors and various distinctions between the teas. I was taking busy notes on Robert. And then as we finished yet another pot, Robert began to ponder the possibility that he would be sourcing Pursuing Pure Perfection's autumn stock of tea on his own this year, constantly on the lookout for Lao Song, with only me to help at best.

After the tea had succeeded in loosening us up, Robert said:

"Those two knobs from Lotus Blossom gave me a good crack to the head. I probably should have got a few stiches, but I didn't ever end up going to the hospital and it's started to heal up quite nicely on its own."

He provided me with the opportunity to examine the crack to his head, which was, in my own non-expert opinion, healing up quite nicely for what it was. Then Robert actually thanked me for running out on him the way I had in Pomasha:

"In fact, it was your hasty, unskilled effort which afforded me the opportunity for escape," he told me with a wink.

Robert then explained how once I had skipped out on the tab at the Pretty Baby Hotel, there had been an involved, but confused, chase in an attempt to corral me. This allowed a small window of time in which Robert could run out through a side door. Then some old East Asian or Indian wisdom kicked in, and Robert hiked double-time back to the tea temple we had visited on the previous day. There, as he told it, he began a pilgrimage of sorts, walking from temple to small tea temple along the towering peaks of the Longshen range. Eventually he made his way to the lamasery overlooking the tiny crossroads town of Pingxing, where he stumbled down the mountain and into town, utterly exhausted, but now far enough away from danger to return to Lime River via more conventional means of transport.

"What an ingenious means of escape!" I glowed as I marveled at Robert's way of thinking.

Robert indicated that there was more to the story and that I should better not interrupt again. So I waited patiently as he spent some time searching out a particular teapot from the jumbled mess beneath the camphor trunk. I was about to give up on hearing the rest, but when the time was right, he resumed:

"When I got back to Lime River, after what must have been a week or two on the road, I was completely spent. I was too agitated to sleep, despite the fact that I was dog-tired. So I sat for many days as I had in the temples and monasteries along the trail until, eventually, I was finally able to get some rest. I just kept thinking: 'Wouldn't it have been awful if I had needed to walk *all the way back* to Lime River!'"

"Where did you sleep on the mountain?" I asked, fixed with great curiosity on the man who had been my greatest model for living an adventurous life abroad.

"I slept on the mats in the temples when they were open—which most of them were—fortunately for me.

"I got some strange looks from the monks here and there, but since I was only ever in each temple for one night, and because the temples on Longshen trail are so remote and the monks are so ascetic, I never ended up drawing too much attention to myself in any one place."

Robert stopped to rinse the teapot, before dumping the water out into a swill pail on the floor.

"Well, that's that," he said. "So here I am."

二十六

Given everything that was going on, I bet you'll believe how happy I was the next evening to go to work with Eight Fortunes. He and I were in the Chinese restaurant on the top floor of the Golden Rooster Hotel and he was treating. The meal itself should have been called the Feast of Yunnan Splendour. It started off with cured ham cubes, fried peanuts, and crispy roast duck. Then out came a round of spicy rice noodles to wash that all down.

The General Manager of the hotel was there. His name was Wu Liaoning. He was corpulent and rubicund, exactly what one would expect from a man who was called upon to entertain at all hours of the night and day, whenever the hotel needed to lend face to an important guest. Liaoning was a celebrity of sorts in town because he was married to the anchor of the local news, the news that was the same on every channel, all the time.

"You're lucky to be able to try *Maotai*," Liaoning whispered in my ear in English.

Eight Fortunes Liu heard and understood and announced boastingly, "I have seven cases of the stuff in my garage!"

Everyone laughed.

＊ ＊ ＊ ＊ ＊

There was a regular businessman there too, to woo Eight Fortunes. He owned a Chinese medicine factory and was looking for investment. His enterprise needed capital to purchase the requisite machinery to expand production to a new line of soap products he endeavored to sell. This being the case, cigarettes were distributed and lit. I got up and toasted the General Manager and Eight Fortunes. Then I went all around the table, cheersing and drinking with everyone.

"Go and sit down," Mr. Liu ordered, once he could see I was already getting pretty drunk.

A course of five locally-produced pork dishes came out from the kitchen with the next two bottles of *Maotai*. And after these delicacies were ravaged and the bottles emptied—and cigarettes passed about and lit—Eight Fortunes Liu sat confidently, *always confidently*, with his shoes off and his socked feet upon the table. And you should know that when Eight Fortunes Liu talked about something, *anything*, he laughed heartily afterwards, no matter the topic or the gravity of the situation:

"How about all those people who died in that [insert name of the latest natural disaster or man-made catastrophe]?"

Then he would laugh his gruff Duozu laugh, never resting his eyes on anyone for long enough to let them get a good look.

＊ ＊ ＊ ＊ ＊

After the Feast of Yunnan Splendour, the Chinese men retreated to a mahjong table for more cigarettes and cards. Not being familiar with the game at hand, I insisted they start without me. I walked over to the full-length window between the gaudy mirrors to look out and over downtown Lime River. I was glad to be above it all, separated by a plate of glass and a long fall from the unwashed weekend masses of East Wind Music Park. Way down there, thousands of people milled about on the dirt paths, admiring the putrid water of the ponds, where goldfish choked for life among the lily pads and floating refuse.

For some time in Lime River, I'd felt as if I were the inhabitant of my own, personal island, somewhere halfway between China and the U.S. But during that fleeting moment in the General Manager's dining room, my thoughts became clear and lucid; my island stretched its legs to both shores and I was home. The underlying language of our hopes and dreams is the same for us all, regardless of nationality or ethnicity or religion or intellect. The collective unconscious is there for us to find, just as it was for Eight Fortunes, and as it had been for the animist ancestors of the Flower-Belt people on their mountain in Longshen Shan. *The collective unconscious should be the starting point for all interhuman interactions and social structures, regardless of any layers of artifice with which mankind has sought to replace it.*

"Small Tiger," Eight Fortunes interrupted, pointing at me and signaling for me to come over.

Several hands had been played quickly, and Eight Fortunes, true to his name, had won them all. Towering piles of pink bank notes sat before him at the gaming table.

"Our cards are really poor tonight," admitted the man who wanted to make the medicinal soap.

"I'm just not as lucky as I was with so-and-so last night," complained Wu Liaoning, before throwing his cards into the center of the table.

Eight Fortunes just laughed his gruff laugh and handed out limited-edition Golden Rooster cigarettes. Then he enticed the man interested in making the medicinal soaps to buy several *tong* of tea from me.

二十七

It was a slow night in Lime River. It was still early, I think, but I was drunk from the hotel, and it was dark and rainy. On my way back to the International Quadrant, I found the door to Pursuing Pure Perfection slightly ajar. A soft light poured from inside the tea shop and out onto the cobblestone street. Robert Painter was inside, sitting at the camphor-laurel trunk. That night was the last time I would see Robert, and had I known this at the time, I may have listened to him more carefully. He was saying: "Every tea has its own flavor, its own set of taste properties—"

He held a clear pouring vessel up to the light for examination.

"It's just like people. Every person has their own flavor, too, wouldn't you agree, Small Tiger? Some are sweet. Some are astringent. Some are a little bitter. People can be sour, too, but Pu'er tea usually isn't—so there's a difference, I guess—but you see my point. And just as we all have preferences for with whom we prefer to spend our time, we all have our own taste in tea. So don't ever let anyone tell you what good tea is and what it is not.

Let your mind be idle and find the taste slowly, on your own terms. Only then will you know what good tea really is."

Having imparted this wisdom unto me, Robert just sort of wilted down behind the stump with satisfaction. He placed a bamboo coaster on the table and rummaged through his collection of tea tools.

"How's Lao Pu?" I asked him.

Robert smiled, using a pair of metal forceps to daintily set a fresh tasting cup before me upon the table.

"Is he doing any better?" I asked, not at all sure what to expect.

"Oh, he's out of the hospital—been out for a few days," Robert assured me. "Lai Sao says he looks younger, has lost weight, and is ready to get back to the tea business."

Robert smiled his all-knowing, Buddha smile as he began a long pour.

"Longshen Shan. Lotus Blossom Village," he announced.

"This is it?" I asked. "This is the magic tea?"

He nodded.

"It's from the amount you were able to smuggle out of the jungle for Lao Pu. He's doing much better now, you know, and I don't think he would mind us having a taste," Robert smiled with a twinkle.

"With no ashes mixed in either this time?" I joked and we both laughed.

Then he looked to me and said, "But first you must smell the tea. Every tea has its own aroma, of course. And it is essential to first judge this aroma according to its own merits, as aroma is a key component of taste."

Robert poured the broth into our tasting cups, pouring first for me, then for himself. We lifted our glasses and wafted the steam towards our noses; it condensed on our faces as we looked at each other and smiled. The aroma was overwhelmingly sweet and earthy, like a piece of you that has been lost your whole life, now found its way back to reunite with your body and with your mind, to call on you and make you whole again. I glanced once more at Robert. He felt it too with his nose buried deeply into his tasting glass, his nostrils nearly submerged in the golden soup.

"This one's for the taste," I said, lifting my cup in salute; and we drank, first one tasting sip and then two, smacking our tongues against the roofs of our mouths.

"Well, what do you think?" Robert asked me.

"It's sweet. And maybe bitter, too. It's sweet on the sides of my tongue and the insides of my cheeks. But it's bitter somewhere else—maybe on the back of my tongue or on the roof of my mouth."

We both took a third sip.

"You sense bitterness?" asked Robert.

"Well, I'm not sure, I think I'll need to drink a few more cups until I get a true feel for its nature."

"Yes, definitely," chuckled Robert. "Of course, you will."

I pressed my tongue to the roof of my mouth, forgetting where I was, breathing in the sweet aroma. I was reminded of cherry pies and of blackberry picking, of swimming among the tree roots and peat in the deepwater lakes of Ohio, of turkey dinners and cranberry sauce, of fresh grapes, of cabernet sauvignon, of tobacco and alfalfa. All of these flavors merged into the perfect whole, a whole no other tea, and no other taste, possessed. This adventure was singular, and no one would ever, or could ever, experience it in the same way ever again.

"Let's do another for the mind and spirit," I suggested to Robert as he began to steep a second pot.

As I said this, he turned to me quite seriously and said:

"But it's never just as simple as that. *It's like life, isn't it?* Just wait until the astringency kicks in. Then you'll have even more to ponder."

＊ ＊ ＊ ＊ ＊

One pot for the taste, one pot for our health, and one for our minds and spirits. We drank until the insides of our mouths became chalky, until our minds were light and giddy.

Eventually, Robert was saying:

"I think it's time we bring out some Yiwu mountain tea. Yiwu is in the eastern tea-growing region of Yunnan. It's a part of the six ancient tea mountains of the Ming Dynasty. The teas from the eastern region are mellower than the ones we've been drinking so far today.

"Longshen Shan, Laobanzhang, Bulang Mountain—they're all relatively western Yunnan in their origin and taste.

"But Yiwu's from the East—from right along the Tea Horse Trail. Let's see if you can spot the differences!"

"I can't spot anything anymore," I protested weakly. "My tongue is confused."

Robert paid me no mind. He continued:

"Eastern Yunnan teas need eastern Yunnan teapots. Western Yunnan teas need western Yunnan teapots."

And so on.

二十八

By the time I got out of the tea shop, it was that dead time of night when everything was still and quiet. The late-night barbecue stands had long been closed, but the tropical songbirds had yet to begin their morning reverie.

I walked the streets back to the Quadrant, and as I did, I passed the short-haul bus station. This was where down-on-their-luck villagers went home to family after a stint in the big city. There were usually a couple of *motos* and a handful of taxis waiting outside, but at this late hour there were none.

At the corner near the station house were two men. I couldn't really make them out in the darkness, but they stood next to a parked Jeep, smoking and speaking to one another in hushed tones of dialect. Soon enough, though, I did indeed recognize them, and when they saw me too, they stopped talking in an instant. One had a keychain latched to his belt loop. The other was a grimy-looking tea merchant.

Skill, the karaoke singer, threw his cigarette to the ground and ejaculated a halt-sounding command. Lao Song, older and less-coordinated, struggled to put out his butt as they both took off after me.

I looked around for witnesses, but there were none. So I kicked off my sandals and turned corners in the opposite direction, hoping that I knew the backstreets of Lime River better than some scumbags from out of town.

I fled, every so often looking over my shoulder to make sure Skill and Lao Song weren't gaining on me. My bare feet ground into the dusty streets of downtown as I began to breathe for maximum efficiency.

In a ploy to lose my foes—and it may not be hyperbole to say *to save my own life*—I turned abruptly into Old Lime River, into the protective maze of alleyways and mud-brick houses and bird cages and vacant fruit stalls.

There, within the meandering backstreets of the large, dark night, the bright moon lit my steps and obscured each dark hiding spot I considered as I passed. I turned another corner—a corner the same as all the rest in Old Lime River—and as I did, the Old City disappeared out from all around me. Gone were the television connections darting seductively into the mud stucco walls. Gone was the Guardian of Nothing. I froze on the edge of a vast construction pit to see the Old City had been razed here to make way for something—a sign called it the Absolute Fortune Center—it was meant to be a block of new luxury apartments and a fashion mall. In the pit below, I could see the giant cranes and huge machines and all the piles of rebar that were anchoring New China's growth. With no other means of escape, and no other hope, I slipped down the dirt embankment and into the belly of the beast.

The white light of the moon led me through that field of rubble, through the wires and the pipes and the graveyard of broken machines. I turned back and was dismayed to see two shadowy figures kicking dirt down the embankment after me. I wish I could admit to courage, but instead I wasted no time in diving headfirst into a sewer pipe to hide.

I cowered there amongst the industrial refuse all that night and into the early morning, waiting, just waiting. I fought to breathe as silently as possible, convinced that Skill and Lao Song were lurking somewhere nearby, checking out every pipe and piece of equipment, searching for me.

With the first ashy hues of dawn—as soon as I heard the tinny-tinny sound of the bicycles starting their morning routes—when I heard the regular call of the woman who announced, "*Spicy, Marinated Eggs for Sale!*" I exited the Absolute Fortune Center—dirty, shoeless, sore and tired.

二十九

On my way back to the International Quadrant that morning, I scanned every corner and kept a constant lookout for anyone who might have been following. I must have looked haggard, because the regulars who started popping up here and there on their morning routes surveyed me with distrust and fear. The fear had ahold of me now, too. There was no shaking that now.

My next adventure was to begin promptly, so I returned to the apartment and decided to bathe. There was no hot water, so I ladled cold water from a basin down my back and to wherever else I could manage. I grabbed some clean clothes and threw them into a backpack. I had no time for all the tea-spattered reflections I've had the luxury to offer in this volume. I was leaving Yunnan, and quickly.

I made two phone calls that morning. One was to Lao Pu. His phone was off. The other was to Eight Fortunes, to let him know I was leaving. And when I exited my apartment in the Quadrant for the last time, the black Audi sedan was waiting for me there at the curb, parked in front of the *moto* men.

Unable to bear the mystery of who was at the helm of the Audi any longer, Che called out to me:

"Where are you headed?"

"Just down the hill for a cup of tea," was my only reply.

The trunk of the Audi popped open and I deposited my sparse belongings inside.

"Going back to be with your parents, right?" Eight Fortunes suggested right away as I stepped in—giving me an easy way out, without having to explain.

"Right," I agreed. "I've probably been away for too long. It's time I went back and looked in on them."

As we pulled away from the curb, Eight Fortunes handed me an envelope with the Golden Rooster Tobacco Group letterhead. He said:

"Here is a ticket to Hong Kong. If anyone asks you, you are doing business on my behalf in Zhuhai." He scanned me confidently, "Once you get to Hong Kong it shouldn't be too difficult to find a plane back to America."

I reached into my pocket. "How much was the ticket?" I asked, feigning to look for a few *kuai*. "How much do I owe you?"

"You don't need to give me any money," offered the third or fourth richest man in Lime River. "Perhaps you can show me around sometime in your country."

I wanted to say more to Eight Fortunes—to explain to him about the magic tea and the knobs from Lotus Blossom Village. But Chinese men don't usually talk to each other like that. This ride to Kunming and the ticket to Hong Kong and all the rest of everything, was already a part of some future transaction, methodically-planned by a master business-man, to be exacted at some indefinite point in the uncertain future. Eight Fortunes just laughed his gruff laugh and made small talk, biding his time and squinting at the road ahead.

So it was like that that we drove off and out of Lime River and toward Kunming and Hong Kong and the world outside. I inhaled a deep breath of the tobacco-scented air and prepared again to become someone else.